AFTERMATH

J. L. Fredrick

Published by
Joel Lovstad-Publishing
701 Henry St.
Waunakee, WI 53597

Printed in the United States of America

ISBN: 0-9749058-2-8

Other Novels by J. L. Fredrick

Another Shade of Gray

Cursed by the Wind

Across the Dead Line

The Other End of the Tunnel

For more information about
titles by J. L. Fredrick,
visit
www.JLFredrick.com

For the Class of '66

CHAPTER 1

"Here's to the graduate."

Don Kelly was never any good at making a toast or long-winded speeches, but he raised his glass to this special occasion -- May 19th, 1966, his son's eighteenth birthday. Shawn would graduate with honors from Westland High School in two weeks. The acceptance letter from Wisconsin University lay neatly folded on Shawn's upstairs bedroom dresser, assuring him of what he wanted most. There was good reason for celebration at the Kellys' country home that night; four glasses clinked together over the table.

Don had offered Shawn a much grander version of this party a week earlier, but the youngster insisted only the people who meant the most to him should attend -- Mom, Dad, and his best friend, Steve. A whole summer full of planned activities would adequately serve as celebrations, but this night, Shawn wanted to be low-keyed and private. He was not one to flaunt his intelligence to gain attention.

Shawn enjoyed his circle of friends with whom he joined occasionally for a softball game or swimming at the lake; the part-time job at his father's lumberyard kept him in focus with reality. He spent much of his free time at the Public Library, as academics had always been his priority, and unlike many, among his generation, Shawn grasped the concept of successful education as the key factor for securing a berth in a prosperous future.

Steve Allison, his best buddy, was one of the very few people who had ever successfully penetrated into Shawn's somewhat private world. They had known each other since elementary school; trust and understanding had built their strong friendship; they shared a passion for cars, baseball and adventure; they highly cherished weekend camping and fishing excursions that afforded them outdoor serenity and valued companionship. They knew their time together would soon be limited, and they were saddened by the thought of it, although, Don Kelly looked forward to it.

On this special night, Shawn's esteemed confidant sat across the table, grinning as though he knew something fantastic was about to happen. As Shawn shoveled in the last forkful of the best lemon cake his Mom had ever made, Don suggested they all go out to the garage, as there was something he wanted Shawn to see. Shawn suspected that it must have some connection with his birthday present, but he was expecting a new wristwatch -- the one he had so subtly dropped hints about during the last month.

Don gave the T-handled latch a twist and lifted the garage door. Shawn's lower jaw dropped as if a ten-pound weight were hooked to it. Frozen with astonishment, his eyes trained on the hand-lettered sign, "HAPPY BIRTHDAY SHAWN," sprawling across the windshield of a metallic moss green '65 Mustang Fastback. Steve stood shoulder-to-shoulder with him.

"Dad checked it over this afternoon, and then I snuck it over here while you were at the library. Whatya think?"

"It's awesome!" were the only words Shawn could get to come out as he stared at the two wide, gleaming white stripes flowing down the center of the hood, and the glistening chrome Mustang medallion nestled in the grille.

Don dangled a set of keys in front of Shawn. "Your Mom and I looked at a half dozen Mustangs before we decided on this one. She's got a 289 V-8 and a four speed... I think you're gonna like it."

"Like it? I *love* it!" Shawn stepped between his Mom and Dad, and hugged them with loving arms. "Thank you... thank you... *thank you!"*

It was Steve's turn to make his presentation. "I know this ain't as exciting as a car... but I got this for you. Happy birthday." He handed Shawn a key ring attached to a gold disc with a galloping stallion logo, identical to the one in the grille of the car.

Shawn put his arm around his best friend's shoulders. "It's perfect. I love it. Thanks Buddy."

This was the best birthday Shawn could remember -- his Dad had surprised him with a shiny new Schwinn Varsity ten-speed bike on his thirteenth birthday, but even that couldn't compare to the magnitude of this event. And Steve's crowning touch couldn't have been more perfect.

Shawn looked at his Dad with excited puppy dog eyes. "Can I take it for a ride? Right now?"

Don beamed with an overwhelming sense of self-satisfaction. He had just made his only son the happiest eighteen-year-old on the planet.

"Sure. It's all gassed up and ready to go... and it's all yours. Just be careful."

Shawn turned to his mother. He knew she had been objecting to her little boy owning a car just yet.

"Thanks, Mom." He gave Kathy Kelly a warm hug. "Ya know, I was really only expecting a watch."

Kathy returned the hug and squeezed out a worried grin.

"I'll be right back," Shawn said to Steve, and then darted into the house. A couple of minutes later, he returned, carrying a spiral notebook.

With a smile as wide as the Mississippi River, Shawn ripped the paper sign from the windshield, opened the driver's door and plopped into the seat. Steve didn't need an invitation to join him. Shawn brought the engine to life with the turn of a key, eased the Mustang out of the garage, and idled it down the driveway. Once on the road, he gently shifted through the gears getting up to speed. He had been driving the lumberyard trucks for nearly two years; mastering the clutch and manual transmission was no difficult task. Only a year old with less than 10,000 miles showing on the odometer, this Mustang was in near showroom new condition; no rattles, squeaks, rust, dents, rips or tears --

just smooth, responsive power at the touch of his toe, and the quick ratio steering and high performance suspension gave it a feel far superior to anything Shawn had ever dreamed of. The only other passenger car he had ever driven, besides the yard trucks, was his Dad's '64 Chrysler New Yorker -- big and luxurious. But *this*. This was pure pleasure. The day just couldn't get any better. Or could it? Steve adjusted the radio to tune in the local station just as The Beach Boys' *Good Vibrations* graced the airwaves. It was Shawn's favorite pop tune; certainly, he must be in Heaven.

Shawn had to stop at the library before it closed at eight o'clock. Sara had promised to proof read the rough draft of his Senior English term paper, due at the end of the week.

During the past four years, Shawn and Sara had established an admirable relationship despite the decades of age difference. She was everyone's friend, but of all the youngsters who passed through the library, Shawn was her favorite. He seemed to fill the void in her life -- the son she never had, and his sponge-like thirst for knowledge certainly didn't hurt, either. She always made herself available to help Shawn with school research projects, no matter how busy she might be at the time, and Shawn had grown fond of her company, as she was one of the few people in Westland who would talk with him on his level when it came to topics other than baseball, cars, or lumber. They had built a mighty bridge over the generation gap, and both traveled it frequently.

Shawn didn't know the dignified, silvery haired man who sat across from Sara at her desk, just inside the old, squeaky-floored Public Library. They were quietly conversing over an object and several pages of notes, both of which Shawn had seen before several times. Sara immediately arose from her chair and greeted Shawn with a warm smile. The gray haired man paid little attention as Shawn and Sara strolled to a reading table across the room. Sara had already conveyed her Birthday wishes earlier that day, so they got right to the business at hand.

"I hope I'm not interrupting anything important. I just wanted to drop off my term paper before you closed."

Sara responded as though it were foolish for Shawn to even think she wouldn't have time for him. "Heavens, no. That's just Professor Taylor from the University of Minnesota. He's here helping me with some research I'm doing on that old artifact I found when I was little. Now, let me take a look at that thesis."

For the first time since the new Schwinn, something took precedence over schoolwork. "Actually, I thought I'd just pick it up again tomorrow. Dad gave me a car for my birthday, and Steve is waiting outside... we're taking it out for a shakedown cruise."

He stood up and motioned to Sara with the enthusiasm of a kid at Christmas.

"C'mon over to the door and take a look."

Sara followed Shawn to the front door, knowing there was no keeping his attention focused on a term paper at a time like this.

"Oh my! It's a beauty. You'll have to come by and give me a ride someday."

"I will... and thank you for going over my paper."

He was at the bottom entrance step when he paused and turned back toward Sara. "Bye, Sara. I'll see you tomorrow." At nearly a dead run he returned to the shiny green Mustang. This was not the time to be thinking about schoolwork.

Shawn slipped into the buckskin colored bucket seat and looked into Steve's eyes. "I really like the key chain... I really do."

Steve pressed his lips together and acknowledged Shawn's sincerity with a nod.

Truly the closest friend Shawn had ever known, Steve Allison was the son of a locally well-known and liked auto mechanic, Richard Allison. They had lived alone for the past six years, as Steve's mother had divorced Richard when Steve was only eleven, and had moved to Michigan with her two younger daughters to live with her new boyfriend. Steve had seen very little of his mother or sisters since then, except for a couple of times when the siblings stayed with them for two weeks during the summer. The relationship with his mother had not been good. His most dominant memories of her were those of neglect, and always taking a back seat to the girls; in their mother's eyes, the sun rose and set on them. Steve was glad he only had to put up with them for a couple of weeks, every couple of years. He was glad, too, that his custody had been placed in his father's hands; Steve liked his Dad, and although they struggled with financial matters and domestic affairs, their personalities rarely clashed.

Steve was handsome, physically well developed and smart, although, his personality tended to hide his intellectual traits from almost everyone except Shawn. A shining reputation didn't exactly follow him: he'd been suspended from school twice – once for smoking in the boys' room, and once for a fight in the hall that he didn't start. Steve possessed that unlucky charm of often being in the wrong place at the wrong time: he took the unjust rap for unsightly, profane spray paint graffiti on a teacher's picket fence, and one night, while roaming the streets alone, a County Deputy wrongly accused him of lighting firecrackers in several darkened back yards, just because Steve had some matches in his shirt pocket.

Steve Allison seemed to be the most misunderstood kid in town; the authorities always found his name on their unwritten list when tracking down pranksters, and for that very reason, Steve felt pressured into a life of recluse.

But Shawn knew there was a good person that no one else saw behind that misunderstood mask. Steve's calm and cool demeanor rarely allowed him to get rattled in the face of any adversity, a characteristic that often became the rock on which Shawn leaned when things got a little tense.

As they cruised the streets of Westland that night, they came to realize their lives were slowly changing, while this quiet little midwestern city with its streets lined with face-lifted buildings dating back to the pioneer days, would more than likely remain just as it was for years to come. It wasn't a bad place to live; Westland's down-home atmosphere, friendly citizens, a total lack of criminal activity, and complete absence of racial slurs, made it quite attractive to those who made their homes there. But Shawn and Steve were advancing by leaps and bounds. How could the community, where they grew up, hold in store the future they desired? That was a question neither of them could answer. When their High School graduation was behind them, they could enjoy their usual summer activities, with one exception: this year, their work schedules might prove to be a bit more rigorous than in the past. A new era was beginning, and they were already missing the old one.

CHAPTER 2

June descended on Westland in all of the radiant beauty that Mother Nature could muster. Abundant sunshine, seasonal southern breezes, and warm spring showers had transformed the countryside from its receding drab, winter remnants, to an Eden of splendor, as if the Gods had dipped their brushes into a surplus of green. Rainbows of color flourished in gardens, and the contoured fields revealed distinct rows of newly planted corn. Sweet clover aroma permeated the air, and the buzzing symphony of lawn mowers, barking dogs, and screaming blue jays filled the day.

Nearly a week had passed since the graduation ceremonies at Westland High. The planet had inherited yet another new crop of eager and able bodies faced with the task of maintaining society. Some would go on to become professional athletes. Some were destined to pursue careers in medicine, education, law, and skilled trades. Many would be content to continue the heritage of the family-owned farms into the future. And in this time of political upheaval on the other side of the globe, the Viet Nam conflict had drawn the United States' intervention, and the Draft Board had many of the young males wondering if their futures included M-14's and rice paddies. Two years earlier, the community had plunged into a state of shock, when it heard the news of one of its own, needlessly dying in a battle of the conflict that it didn't understand. Jerry Krueger's untimely demise was still fresh in the minds of everyone -- especially the teen-aged boys registering with the Selective Service on their eighteenth birthdays.

A few of Shawn's classmates had trekked off to far away places like

Belvedere, Illinois, hoping to secure assembly line jobs at the new Chrysler-Plymouth factory. Some of the unsuccessful ones had already returned, disappointed, joining the ranks of others seeking local employment. Some were preparing for their annual family vacation trips. The less ambitious youngsters were just hanging out, providing subject matter for gossip-inspired conversation among the senior citizens, gathered on park benches and in coffee shops.

Shawn and Steve, though, were already engaged in part-time jobs, built-in by virtue of a family tree.

Shawn was assured, as the only child of a successful businessman, to step into his father's shoes, just as his father had done, although, he wasn't quite sure that an entire lifetime of two-by-fours, shingles, and ten-penny nails was what he really wanted. But there were other advantages: not only was he the sole heir to his father's lumber dynasty, Shawn had always enjoyed the benefits of his parents' total devotion, in the absence of siblings demanding equal shares of attention. The Mustang, and an imminent college career, at his father's expense, was solid, physical evidence of that. And college afforded him protection from the draft.

Steve knew exactly what he wanted. But what he wanted greatly opposed what was feasible. A degree in Mechanical Engineering had been his dream for quite some time, but he had always kept that a well-guarded secret, even to Shawn. Steve was concerned about his father's embarrassment of feeling financially inadequate, unable to afford college expenses. He realized, at best, that he would probably settle for a two-year trade school, only after working a year in order to save enough money to finance the venture on his own. And of course, there was the draft, from which he had no sheltering defense, and perhaps, Uncle Sam would be making his decisions for him, long before he arrived at any college campus.

Steve's father would take over the automotive service business from its retiring owner within a few months. Richard Allison had worked at Edgar's Service Center for fifteen years, and there was little doubt in anyone's mind that he would still be there for another fifteen years, as the proprietor. Steve, too, was assured of a future there, if he chose to make Westland his permanent domicile. But much like Shawn, uncertainty of a lifetime in Westland posed limitations in his quest of an ultimate goal. His attention had been captured by names like Richard Petty, 'Fireball' Roberts, and Mario Andretti, and cities like Darlington and Daytona sounded more appealing.

****

It was Thursday night. After almost a week of working half days at Kelly Lumber, Shawn had set aside the intense pursuit of scholastic endeavors. Instead of his usual nightly school-year routine of spending an hour or two at the Public Library, that night he and Steve would be in the back stall of Edgar's, where they had been every night that week, engaged in a labor of love. Late last summer, they had constructed a fence for a local farmer, and as compensation for their efforts, they had agreed to be the recipients of a two-tone blue '56 Chevy hardtop. Months earlier, while hiking to a favorite fishing hole, they had spotted it behind a barn, and overgrown in weeds. The old car had been parked behind Edgar's ever since, receiving only occasional attention from its new owners. But now was the perfect opportunity to sire a second chance for the classic. Richard was offering his guidance with the project, but he was reluctant to perform any of the actual work, as he continually encouraged the boys to learn by doing. He would provide the unsupervised after-hours use of the shop and any tools they needed, as long as they respected his workplace and didn't abuse the privileges he was extending to them.

Shawn rounded the corner at the library; he noticed the old building was dark inside. He glanced at his watch -- 8:15 -- Sara had left five minutes earlier, just as she had every night at 8:10 sharp. It was a twenty-minute walk to her house, another of Sara's regimens Shawn knew well. He had accompanied her many times in the past, walking his Schwinn on the route that never varied. Although Steve would be waiting for him at Edgar's, it seemed like a good time to give Sara the promised ride in the Mustang, and perhaps he could chauffeur his highly respected friend, at least half the distance, to her house on the outskirts of town.

As he slowly drove up to the darkened house, Shawn thought it was impossible that he could have missed Sara along the way. It did seem odd that she might have altered her route, but whatever the reason, her ride in the Mustang would have to wait until another time

Steve was already preparing for an evening of tinkering as Shawn eased his steed up to the back door of the large steel building. He recalled how he and Steve used to *tune up* their bicycles out behind the old, rickety two bay service station that once stood there. The original Edgar's was totally destroyed by a fire in 1963, and now, the bold replacement, five times the size of its predecessor, housed an auto repair center, second to none.

While they pushed the old Chevy inside, Shawn's concern for Sara grew.

"I'm worried about Sara."

"Why's that?" Steve asked.

"The library was dark, and so was her house... I followed the exact route she always takes, but I didn't see her."

Steve sensed his friend's concern. "Maybe she had to stop at the store before she went home."

"That's what I thought at first, too, but tonight is Thursday. All the stores close early on Thursday... whatya say we take a little ride? I wanna check one more time."

With the garage doors shut and locked, they jumped into the Mustang, and headed off in search for the missing librarian. Steve suggested checking the library first. "Maybe she could've tripped and fallen before she got to the front door."

Shawn parked in the street in front of the library and ran to the entrance. It was locked. That meant Sara had left the building. It was part of her nightly routine – she never locked the front door until she left for home.

Once more, Shawn drove the exact route that Sara walked every night. If he had missed her before, certainly there would be lights burning at her house by now. But the house was still dark. He ran to her front porch and pounded on the screen door.

"Sara," he called out, but there was no answer.

Complete darkness had swallowed up the neighborhood. Steve leaned against the front fender of the Mustang; he watched Shawn scurry off to the nearest neighbor's house, about thirty yards away. He could see Shawn talking to the resident in the light of the front door, but he couldn't hear the conversation. As quickly as Shawn had run off, he returned and said nothing as he sprinted to the house on the other side. And again he returned with no results from that inquiry.

"Something has happened to Sara... I just know it," Shawn said. He was in near panic.

"Why are you so worried?" Steve asked. "She's probably at some other friend's house somewhere."

"Not likely," Shawn returned. "Sara doesn't see well after dark. I just know she wouldn't be roaming around to the neighbors after dark."

They got in the car and started back toward town. Along the stretch of poorly lit street where there were no houses, Steve caught sight of something bright colored, nearly concealed by the tall grass and weeds in the roadside ditch.

"Stop! Back there! There was something in the weeds."

Shawn locked up the brakes and the Mustang came to a screeching halt. The rear tires squealed again as Shawn backed up to where Steve told him to stop. He set the parking brake, threw open his door and ran around the car, down into the ditch. There lay Sara, motionless; her turquoise dress was torn and stained, and her face was badly bruised.

Shawn kneeled down beside her. "Sara! What happened? Can you hear me?"

Sara was barely conscious and could hardly speak, but she recognized Shawn's voice. "He took my purse... but it's not in there... Shawn, you must get it and keep it." She struggled to get the words out with a mere whisper, her voice scratchy and weak.

Shawn had no idea what she meant. Right then, it seemed more urgent to get help... and fast. Steve didn't need any instructions; he was already in the Mustang and off to find Jake, the City Police Chief. At this time of night, Jake was apt to be around the downtown area and not hard to find.

Shawn removed his shirt, wadded it up and slipped it under Sara's head for a pillow. "Just hang on Sara... Steve'll be right back with some help." He had never experienced such an encounter before -- he really didn't know what to do. He could tell Sara was losing consciousness, and she wasn't breathing well. He was scared like he had never been scared before.

The seconds seemed like hours. All attempts to get Sara to mutter anything at all – just so he'd know she was still alive – rendered nothing. She had completely lost consciousness when Shawn heard the roar of the engines and the two pairs of headlights popped into sight. Jake stopped his squad car in the middle of the lane, red lights flashing atop the roof. Quickly assessing the situation, he recognized the need for assistance of a nearby patrolling County Deputy Sheriff, returned to the car and reached for the two-way radio microphone. Most of the County squads were station wagons that doubled as ambulances in cases of extreme emergency, and this was definitely one of those times when it wouldn't be practical to wait for the nearest ambulance service to arrive from twenty miles away.

Shawn paid little attention to the spoken words, but a feeling of relief flooded him just knowing a clear radio response meant help was not far away.

Jake hustled back to the road ditch. "What happened?" he asked.

"I don't know. We just found her like this. Someone must've..." Shawn stopped in mid sentence.

Jake looked into Shawn's eyes with detective-like curiosity. "Must've what?"

"Well... just before she passed out, she told me that someone took her purse. Maybe she was attacked and robbed."

That comment took Jake by surprise. Until that moment, he had assumed that Sara had merely taken a bad fall, but now the situation took on a whole different appearance. Was this just an accident scene, or that of a violent crime?

In a short time, the County Deputy arrived, followed by a State Trooper and yet another County officer. At least a dozen curious onlookers had gathered like insects attracted to a light. Sara was carefully put on a gurney, loaded into the ambulance that soon sped away with red lights flashing and siren wailing.

There didn't seem to be a clear line of communication between the police officers. The State Patrolman began closely inspecting the front of Shawn's car with a flashlight -- he assumed the vehicle had struck Sara. The second County Deputy was illuminating the interior of the Mustang with his flashlight, but there was nothing to find. Jake continued to search the immediate area hoping to discover the missing purse, discounting Shawn's earlier remark, but he came up with nothing. Although the other two officers suspected Shawn of trying to cover up some wrongdoing, Jake knew the boy and his family too well to believe such accusations. He concurred that Shawn did spend a lot of time at the library with Sara, and that they were good friends, despite a drastic difference in their ages. It didn't seem unusual at all that Shawn would be concerned about Sara's safety and would have been looking for her. Jake abruptly came to Shawn's defense, convincing his counterparts there was no reason to detain the boys any longer -- written statements could be obtained the next day, if necessary.

As Jake sent Shawn and Steve on their way, one thought was nagging at him -- Steve had never come forth after returning to the scene, as if he were avoiding becoming involved. It seemed a little odd, but that was an issue to be addressed at a later time.

The mood for working on the car slithered away, and it *was* getting late. The '56, once again, was returned to its usual outside resting spot, tools put away, and garage doors locked. Shawn's father was in Rapid City, South Dakota, meeting with the owners of several lumber mills, the source of much of the product in Kelly Lumber's inventory. He wouldn't return until the next night, and Shawn's mother was visiting relatives in Missouri for two weeks. Shawn had previously planned to invite Steve to spend that night at their country home, and now, the thought of an overnight companion seemed even more comforting. It would certainly help ease the tension. Steve didn't hesitate to accept the invitation, as he, too, was beginning to feel the effects of the grim situation. His library encounters with Sara hadn't been as extensive, but he understood Shawn's concern, and he wanted to be there for his best friend.

The next morning, after delivering a dish of *Alpo* and a pan of water to the back porch for Duke, the family cocker spaniel, Shawn joined Steve at the kitchen table; they sipped from tall glasses of orange juice, and munched on toast with peanut butter. The visions of Sara's battered face haunted Shawn, and he couldn't stop thinking about the only words she had struggled to speak. He realized he had withheld from Jake part of Sara's last and only statement.

Shawn was faced with some puzzling questions: what, exactly, did she mean by *it* not being in the purse, and why should he find and keep *it?* Should he tell Steve? Or anyone, for that matter. After some self-debating, he determined Steve's camaraderie might be helpful, and convinced him to keep their secret -- at least until they could figure out *what the secret really was.*

As usual, Shawn was scheduled to work at the lumberyard that afternoon. He always jokingly referred to his time there as his "board meetings," but that day he was far removed from making jokes. His agenda included nothing beyond a trip to the hospital to see Sara. Perhaps she would be awake again; she would certainly enjoy his visit, and maybe she could provide an explanation of the curiosity plaguing his wits. Steve declined to ride along; his Dad had the whole day planned with a list of odd jobs Steve was to perform around the shop.

Shawn dropped Steve off at Edgar's and drove toward the hospital. He hated visiting people in a hospital. It wasn't that he didn't care about the well-being of others, or that he was insensitive to their unpleasant conditions and, perhaps, loneliness – he just didn't like hospitals. He'd never been confined in one, and he hoped that he never would. But he knew what he had to do.

For the entire seven-mile drive, his feelings were captured in a cesspool of guilt; he blamed himself for Sara's injuries. He couldn't stop thinking about how he had been too late to pick her up at the library – if only he had been ten minutes earlier, Sara would not be struggling for her life.

"I'm here to see Sara Fremont," Shawn said to the receptionist.

The woman behind the desk responded only with an artificial smile and began thumbing through a stack of papers. When she seemed to locate the information, she looked up at Shawn and frowned. "I'm sorry, but Sara Fremont isn't here anymore."

"Where is she? Did they send her home already?"

"No… her injuries were too severe for this hospital to administer proper treatment. She was transferred to trauma care at the UW Hospital in Madison at four o'clock this morning."

"Well, is she gonna be okay?"

"All I can tell you is that she was in a deep coma, and I don't have any other information."

Shawn fought with an uncontrollable urge to cry. He turned away from the desk and walked slowly to the exit door. His feelings of guilt escalated with every step.

CHAPTER 3

Jake, the middle-aged, stocky-built, always-smiling Chief of Westland's one-man police department, wheeled the brand new Ford Galaxy squad car into the lumber storage yard, as he often did. The other yard hands greeted Jake as he got out of his car. There seemed to be no doubt about the nature of Jake's visit; they knew of Sara's misfortune, and that Shawn had discovered her injured body. They pointed the Chief in Shawn's direction.

Shawn was well acquainted with Jake; his father and Jake had been friends for years, and Jake had been making social visits to the Kelly home for as long as Shawn could remember. Don Kelly and the Chief shared a coffee break at the restaurant nearly every morning. But Shawn understood Jake's business side, as well. Jake could be somewhat intimidating at times, and every youngster in town, including Shawn, knew that staying on Jake's good side was in their best interest. Everyone liked and respected Jake, although, the county deputies often underestimated his abilities in perception.

Jake's slow and deliberate pace across the yard brought a few extra beads of sweat trickling down Shawn's forehead. Shawn knew Jake wasn't there to show off the new car, nor was this just a social visit. He'd never been in any trouble with the law, and he knew he wasn't now, either, but a little guilt tremor still rumbled around in his gut. Shawn had never felt intimidated by Jake's presence, but he knew why this visit made his skin crawl; Jake would present more questions, and Shawn was about to withhold any information regarding the *secret*.

"Shawn, I need your written statement about last night." Jake spoke softly, but with intensity.

Shawn pressed his lips together, closed his eyes and nodded.

"Seems it's more serious now," Jake added. "Sara is--"

"I know," Shawn interrupted. "I went to the hospital this morning." He stared at the ground and pawed at the gravel beneath his feet.

He knew it was probably wrong, but his decision would stand: he would not disclose the entirety of Sara's last words. Sara had entrusted *him* with something that still remained a puzzle; it was his honorable duty to carry out the wishes of a dear friend, and to protect a guarded secret. He needed some time to figure *it* out; he'd find a way to justify the omission, if it became necessary. Every other detail, though, was carefully recalled and jotted down on Jake's clipboard.

Jake scanned over the page. "Okay, Shawn. I'll be in touch," he said. "And I'll let you know if I hear anything about Sara's condition."

Jake marched back to the squad car. A strange, curious sensation poked at Shawn like a sharp dagger as he watched Jake drive away. Jake hadn't been his usual talkative self, like he, too, was holding something back.

All afternoon, Shawn was preoccupied with curious speculations. What did Sara possess that carried so much importance to her? And why would anyone want to steal it from her? Perhaps her statement had just been a delirious reaction caused by the trauma? No. She had spoken Shawn's name; she *knew* he was there with her; she had struggled too hard to utter the not-so-precise instructions.

Sara had always seemed a modest person, leading a life of simple pleasures, and never flaunted money, jewelry or pretentious aims. And there was absolutely no one who could possibly hold any animosities to such a degree -- she didn't even collect the fees for a late book return. It just didn't seem possible that a woman in her late fifties with the meager income of a librarian could become the target of a brutal criminal act.

Then, like prodding a glowing ember in a campfire, the sparks came fluttering out and the flame exploded into reality. Like the sudden impact of a wrecking ball, Shawn crashed through the barrier that had been hiding the answer to the mystery. *It* hadn't dawned on him until that very moment, but now *it* surfaced into plain, clear view.

He darted across the yard and into the building, through the showroom and to where his dad's office door could be closed behind him. He plopped into his dad's chair and quickly reached for the phone, dialing the number he knew, without even thinking about it.

"Edgar's Service," the familiar voice answered on the other side of town.

"Hello… Richard?"

"Hi, Shawny." Richard was the only person who ever tailed his name with a *Y* but coming from him, Shawn always thought it was kind of cool. And Richard always treated Shawn like a prince, appreciating the friendship the boys shared. Any other time, Shawn would have paused to absorb some of the royal treatment.

"Is Steve there?"

"He's not here, Shawny. I sent him after parts. He should be back around five, or so."

"Will you please tell him to come out to my house when he gets back? I really need to talk to him right away. I should be home by five-thirty."

"Sure thing, Shawny. I'll tell him."

****

Steve's pure white '59 Chevy Impala pulled into the driveway at 6:30. He had inherited the car from his grandfather, but he rarely drove it. "Hi, Buddy. What's goin' on?" he asked as he entered the kitchen.

Shawn was excited. His words shot out like lead from a machine gun. "I know now what *it* is and I need your help to get it before someone else does... I think I know where it is."

Steve's eyes squinted in a confused stare. "Whoa! Slow down before you rupture something." He put a hand on Shawn's shoulder and urged him to sit down at the kitchen table.

"Sara found this old artifact when she was a little girl," Shawn started again. His whole body blazed with excitement. "She's kept it all these years, and she's been doing a lot of research on it. I've seen her studying it at the library for a couple of years, now. I think she must have found something pretty fantastic, 'cause somebody else wants it, too... bad enough to do what they did to her."

What had really happened to Sara had not yet been confirmed, and Steve wasn't convinced that Shawn was completely on track with this theory. "How do you know that's what happened? How do you know that it wasn't just an accident?"

"I don't know, for sure. But I do know Sara never carried much cash, and I *do* know what she said to me, and I don't think she would have said that if it wasn't something important."

"So what's your plan?" Intrigue was drawing Steve in.

"The artifact is in a desk drawer in the library... somehow, we have to get in there."

Steve started deducing the possibilities from another perspective. "But if it really was a mugger, he has Sara's purse -- *and* her keys. What's stopping him from gettin' into the library?"

"Nothing."

"He may have already been there and taken the artifact," Steve suggested.

Shawn stared deeply into the tablecloth, searching for all the possible remedies. "On the other hand, maybe he hasn't. Maybe he would wait for a more opportune time. Or maybe he doesn't know exactly where to look for it yet."

Steve agreed with Shawn's speculations. He gave a crooked little grin and nodded. All of Shawn's observations were the very reason why they had to take action -- and soon.

"There's got to be extra keys somewhere," Steve said.

Shawn just listened with a curious stare.

"And everyone knows you spend a lot of time at the library. Why don't you just ask Jake to get you the keys?"

Shawn thought about that idea, but quickly rejected it. "The way Jake acted today, I think the cops would really be suspicious if we ask to get into the library. As far as they know, the only thing in the library is books. And besides... they're not gonna let a couple of kids in there without supervision... I'd never have a chance to look through her desk if someone else was there."

"So what other choice do we have?" Steve asked, knowing what Shawn would propose.

"We've got to get in some other way, without anyone knowing." Shawn paused and threw out a devilish smile. "We'll have to break into the library."

Don Kelly arrived home a little earlier than Shawn expected. He was exhausted after the near nonstop ten-hour drive.

The boys straightened up at the table and tried to act as if this were just an ordinary visit.

"Hi, Dad. How was your trip?'

"Long and tiring," Don replied. He stared at Steve for a long moment and then turned to his son with one of his disciplinary looks. "We've got six extra semi-loads of lumber coming Monday. I want you there early tomorrow... so don't stay up too late tonight."

Shawn's spirit sank to somewhere below the basement. It was Friday night, but he knew there was no convincing Dad he *had* to go out. The library would have to wait until the next night.

"Steve and I are goin' to the ball game tomorrow night," Shawn said quickly, before any more plans could be made for him. "And then we're gonna camp overnight at the lake... okay?"

"I suppose that's okay." Don was too tired to invent any objections. "Now, I'm pretty beat. I'm gonna lie down for a while."

The two boys hustled outside to the driveway. Nearly whispering, as if someone could be listening, they plotted the Saturday night caper.

"We can get in through one of the windows in the rear," Shawn said.

"But those windows are ten feet up," Steve protested.

"I can stand on your shoulders… I'll reach… easy."

"Yeah, I guess that'll work. And it *is* pretty dark back there."

"I'll pry the window open and climb in. You can wait out back and stand watch."

"Gonna be pretty dark in there."

"I know the inside of the library as well as my own bedroom," Shawn said with confidence. "And I'll have a flashlight."

"We *could get caught,* ya know," Steve said.

"The Mustang will be parked on the other side of the trees behind the library. If somebody comes, you run to the car and take off… I'll be okay."

Steve shrugged his shoulders.

"But that's not gonna happen. It'll be simple."

Steve thought a few moments. "Then we should drive over to the ball game so everyone will see us there."

"Good idea," Shawn said. "It'll be the perfect alibi."

"And there'll be lots of kids down at the lake too."

"Right… we'll be able to account for the whole night."

It seemed to be an excellent plan -- one that they hoped would successfully produce the results they were seeking.

Shawn couldn't sleep. He tossed and turned as a thousand visions raced through his head: Will the window open? Will the artifact be where he had last seen it? Is Sara okay? What will happen if they get caught? What kind of trouble could he be getting his best friend into? Who else is after the artifact? He lay as still as possible with eyes closed, desperately trying to induce slumber, but it just didn't work. The minutes kept ticking away. The lighted dial on the clock radio beside his bed displayed 1:47, and he was still wide-awake. Without turning on any lights, he tiptoed down the stairs and into the kitchen, poured a glass of orange juice in the light of the open refrigerator, pulled back a chair and sat at the table. Images of the next night's anticipated escapade still rushed through his mind like a thundering herd of wild stallions. He was so engrossed in the would-be events that he didn't notice his father reaching for the light switch. Shawn squinted as the overhead fluorescent fixture made its strobe-like entrance, emerging the room from darkness.

"Why the hell are you sitting here in the dark... in your underwear?"

Don Kelly was a man of strong ethical values -- both in business and personal life. He had inherited Kelly Lumber Company from his father, who had nurtured the entrepreneurship from a small water-driven sawmill on the banks of a near-by stream in the 1930's, to its present-day retail status, located near the heart of this thriving agricultural community. Don had spent nearly his whole life learning the values of hard work and dedication as his father's right hand man, unlike his only brother, Andy, who drifted away from the family, and soon lost all rights to any legal ownership of the business. Kelly Lumber was willed solely to the loyal son, Don, and Andy turned to alcohol as a gesture of rebellion. It was only Don's influence with the School Board that secured Andy's present janitor position at Westland High. And it remained to be seen if Andy's past history of short-term employments could be surpassed with any longevity at the school.

Not only had Don Kelly become a pillar of the community and a successful businessman, he cared deeply about his family; he was dedicated to providing the best life for them within his means, even if it meant sacrifices of his own pleasures. A quick survey of their modern, nicely appointed country home, and their comfortable lifestyle, showed evidence that he was not experiencing much difficulty in maintaining that ideal.

In a shaky, nervous, low tone, Shawn responded to his father's inquiry. "Couldn't sleep. Guess I'm worried about Sara." It was then he realized his Dad probably knew nothing about the incident, and he proceeded to explain -- everything except the part about the artifact. He was careful not to reveal even the tiniest shred of information about it. They talked on and on, about other topics, as well -- Shawn's upcoming trip to college, the lumber yard, the Mustang, and the phone call Shawn had received from his mother. The Kelly father and son had always managed a good line of communication, but it wasn't often they had the opportunity to talk like this.

It seemed to be a good time for Shawn to deploy a question that had been on his mind for at least four years, but had never found the courage to get it off his chest.

"Dad... why don't you like Steve?"

Don had never spoken badly about Steve, but he had never expressed any great love for his son's best buddy, either. He tolerated Steve, and allowed his presence in their home. Although he didn't ever openly voice any objections to the friendship, he secretly disapproved of Shawn's closeness to Steve. Shawn only wished there could be a good relationship between them -- like he enjoyed with Richard.

"What makes you think I don't like Steve?" Don knew that Shawn was uneasy with the question, and was obviously seeking an honest answer.

Shawn chose his words carefully, as to avoid any confrontation. "Well... I guess it's just a feeling. It's the way you act when he's around. He's been my best friend since grade school... but you hardly ever talk to him at all. His Dad's a really cool guy, and you like *him*, don't you?"

Don was backed into a corner, but his son deserved that honest answer. "Sure I do. He's the best mechanic in town, and he's a good guy. But he's divorced -- and Steve hasn't exactly had the best upbringing, and you have to admit... he's not the smartest guy in the world, and you *know* his reputation. I guess I've just always been apprehensive about his influence on you."

"But Dad! It's not Steve's fault his parents are divorced. And who do you think keeps their house clean and washes their clothes and cooks most of their meals? Richard works ten -- sometimes twelve hours a day. He sure doesn't have time for all that. But to see their house, you'd never know it. And Steve really is smart... he'd like to go to college, but Richard probably can't afford it 'cause everything he makes goes to his lazy-ass ex-wife. I feel kinda bad for Steve 'cause he's not able to go to school... he'd make a good mechanical engineer... he's really good at that kind of stuff."

There were other points Shawn could have brought up regarding influence -- like the fact that Steve had never smoked a cigarette until Shawn had coaxed him to try it; and how Steve had never uttered a single word of profanity until Shawn started using language that would have had him licking a bar of soap, had his mother heard it. But he thought it to be in his best interest not to mention any of that.

Don stared at the table, then up at the clock on the wall. "Maybe I've misjudged Steve a little... and maybe I've misjudged my own son, as well." He glanced back up at the clock, deliberately ending the conversation. "Look at the time... it's almost three. We've got a busy day tomorrow. We'd better get to bed."

Shawn felt a sense of relief. He wasn't exactly sure what his Dad's statement about misjudgment meant -- whether he now thought more of Steve, or, less of his own son, but at any rate, it took his mind off all the other turmoil -- at least long enough to let him fall asleep.

****

The hot morning sun flooded Shawn's bedroom. The clock radio clicked to 8:00 just as the deejay was blurting a brief outlook on the impending weather:

> *"Looks like it's going to be a great weekend for the baseball tournament in Westland. Temperatures will soar into the eighty's today, but it should cool down to about seventy degrees by the time the games start tonight at seven-thirty, and there's no sight of rain for the entire weekend. ...And in the news... the pedestrian, apparently struck by an unknown motorist Thursday night in Westland is still in a coma and listed in critical condition at the UW Hospital... according to the Sheriff's Department, the accident is under investigation."*

The radio report about Sara's misfortune caught Shawn off-guard. This shed a different light on his speculations of what might have happened to her. Maybe it *was* just an accident, but why had she instructed him to find and protect the mysterious artifact? This wasn't going to change his mind to pursue that answer.

Morning had come much to quickly, but Shawn had recovered from many late-night study sessions in the past, and he could certainly do the same this day. There were too many tasks to accomplish, and no time to be tired.

A hasty shower and a tall glass of cold orange juice revived a perky spirit. As he bounded out the back door, he saw that his Dad had already provided Duke's morning cuisine, and he headed around the corner of the house to where the Mustang awaited the command to start engines.

The familiar red and white Chevy pickup truck with *Kelly Lumber* lettered on each door, and the shiny, dark blue police car sat poised, bumper-to-bumper, in front of Bergen's Café -- Don and the Chief were partaking of their usual early morning coffee break. Shawn couldn't think of a good reason to stop. He already knew what had to be done, and the sooner he got to the yard, the sooner it would all be finished.

CHAPTER 4

Every Saturday morning, Woodrow Taylor sat at a table on the back patio of his luxurious mansion overlooking the Mississippi River just south of Minneapolis, reading the newspaper and sipping freshly brewed tea. Taylor was a long-time archaeology professor at Minnesota State University. His wife had left him years ago, unable to tolerate his eccentric, self-centered, and greedy ways. Nowadays, he spent the majority of his free time alone in the mammoth dwelling filled with countless rare artifacts, antiques, sculptures, and paintings -- literally a museum of world history.

Two able-bodied but failing University students were in his employ to maintain the park-like estate and the expansive villa. Tommy and Curtis were the only outsiders to ever enter the premises, as Taylor was quite protective of his treasure-filled home. Over the past year, they had earned Taylor's trust with their loyalty to him, in hopes it would increase their chances of a graduation.

A small news brief headline caught Taylor's eye:

LIBRARIAN VICTIM OF HIT-RUN

The short article proved even more interesting as he read on.

> *Sara Fremont, 58, remains in a coma and listed as critical resulting from injuries she sustained as the victim of a hit and run Thursday evening while walking near her home in Westland. Fremont is employed as the librarian in the city's Public Library. Authorities are withholding further details pending investigation.*

"Oh my. What a tragedy," he mumbled. "But what a fortunate opportunity for Woodrow Taylor." His ostensible personality shifted into high gear. Without any hesitation he went to his office, found a University phone directory, and quickly dialed the number.

"Custodial Services... Harold speaking."

"Harold, this is Professor Taylor, Archaeology."

"Yes, Mr. Taylor. What can I do for you?"

"Do you remember Andy, the janitor who used to work in my building? He left about six months ago to take a position at a small-town high school."

"Yeah... Andy Kelly. Yeah, I remember him. What--"

"Thank you very much," Taylor interrupted, and immediately hung up the receiver. He wasn't much for pleasantries with anyone, much less a janitor.

****

Wishing he had taken the phone off the hook before he went to bed, Andy Kelly stumbled from the bedroom of his small apartment above the downtown hardware store. Jack Daniels still had a prominent influence on his navigational abilities, and he wasn't sure how he had gotten home from the Bowling Alley Bar the previous night.

"Hello?"

"Is this Mr. Andrew Kelly?"

"Yeah."

"I am Professor Woodrow Taylor of the Minnesota State University. Do you remember me?"

Andy immediately remembered the snooty, gray-haired professor who had always found fault with his custodial performance. He wasn't going to be concerned with politeness to this son-of-a-bitch. "Yeah... whatya want?"

"I read of the tragic accident involving Sara Fremont in the paper this morning."

"Well, I don't know any more about that than you do, Doc."

"Mr. Kelly! Miss Fremont was... is... a dear friend. I visited her library not more than a month ago. She has in her desk drawer an artifact that I need for study. I am wondering if you could possibly obtain it for me."

"I don't know..."

"For a fee of... say... five thousand dollars?"

CHAPTER 5

By four o'clock, the storage yard beside Kelly Lumber was nearly ready to accept the Monday delivery. Shawn squatted down with his back resting against a stack of two-by-fours, taking advantage of the little bit of shade it was providing, and consuming large gulps from a can of Coke.

Just barely in his line of vision, he spotted Jake's police car partially blocking the gated entrance marked DELIVERIES. The Chief strolled toward him, but Shawn didn't attempt to make eye contact; he just stared down at the ground, wondering if this visit would deliver good news or bad. The gravel crunched louder with each step. Jake's shiny black shoes were all Shawn saw of him as he continued to stare downward, waiting for Jake to speak.

"Hi, Shawn."

Shawn looked up. "Hi Jake." He could sense from Jake's tone that he was troubled. "Have you heard anything about Sara?"

Jake pulled a pack of Camels from his breast pocket, tapped one out and lit up. "She's still in a coma. The doctors say her scull is fractured and there's definite brain damage."

Shawn returned his stare to the gravel.

"From her injuries," Jake went on, "they think she must've been hit by a car. It was probably a side view mirror that caught the small of her back. When she fell to the ground, she hit her head on the pavement. Makes sense -- there isn't a sidewalk out there, so she was probably walking in the street."

Shawn tried to cover his emotion, slowly rising, and stood beside Jake. "Ya know? I could sure use one of those right now."

Jake held the cigarette pack in front of Shawn.

"No -- I can't. My Dad is right over there."

Jake looked into the boy's teary eyes. "You think your old man doesn't know you have a smoke now and then?"

"No -- at least I don't think so." Shawn struggled with another emotional moment.

Jake's serious tone returned. "Shawn... is there anything more you can tell me about what happened Thursday night?"

"N--no... I've told you everything I know."

"We never did find her purse, ya know."

"What do you think? That I took it?"

"No, Shawn, I don't think you'd do a thing like that."

"Well, what then?"

"What about Steve Allison? Do you think he could've done it?"

"Why would he...? NO! He *didn't.*"

Suspicions of Steve's involvement had been growing among the investigating officers, and now Jake was attempting to bait a hook. He knew Shawn and Steve were close friends, and perhaps he could get Shawn to induce some furtive actions, which would be closely watched.

"Sara cashed her paycheck at the bank at 11:45 that morning," Jake explained. "The teller said she took a hundred and fifty dollars in cash. From there she went right to work -- in fact I saw her unlocking the front door of the library just before noon when I was on my way home for lunch. So she had at least that much -- maybe more -- in her purse when she walked home that night."

"So? How could Steve have known that? How does that make him guilty?"

"The bank teller said that Richard and Steve Allison were next in line behind her."

Shawn was quick to come to his friend's defense. "But I was with him that night -- I *know* he didn't do it."

"But according to your statement, you met Steve at the garage *after* you had covered her walking route once without seeing her. It had already happened. You, or he, can't account for his time before you arrived at the garage."

Shawn was in shock. He didn't know what to say. The scene on that dark street flashed before his eyes; he tried desperately to recreate every second and every movement he and Steve had made, but his concern for Sara that night had kept his focus on her – not Steve. He couldn't recall any of Steve's actions, other than watching him drive away in the Mustang.

"And you said it was Steve that spotted Sara's body in the weeds," Jake added. "Sounds maybe like he knew right where to look."

They stood there for a few seconds without speaking. Jake dropped the half-burned cigarette on the ground and stepped on it. "If you think of anything at all, you know where to find me." He walked back to his car, opened the driver's door, and glanced back at Shawn, only to see him motionless, staring at the ground.

Don Kelly was just finishing a conversation with a customer, and walked over to Shawn. "Everything okay?" he asked, for the lack of anything better to say. Shawn looked up at his Dad. "He didn't do it. Steve didn't hurt Sara." He abruptly turned away and went back to scooping up a pile of trash he had swept together before Jake had arrived.

****

Kelly Lumber Company was situated across the street from a central city park that occupied nearly a whole block at the south end of the business district. It wasn't unusual to see Jake's squad car parked at one end of the park under the shade of the lofty oak trees – a perfect vantage point where he could keep an eye on much of the downtown area, and observe would-be traffic violators. His attention, though, was directed toward the small parking lot beside Kelly Lumber and a green Mustang. About ten minutes had passed when Sheriff Barnett's unmarked brown Chevy Bel Aire pulled up along side. Jake and the Sheriff exchanged greetings.

"Anything going on here?" the Sheriff asked.

Jake glanced toward the lumberyard. "I just talked to the Kelly boy about fifteen minutes ago. I put the bug in his ear."

"Think he'll tip off Allison?"

"My guess is that'll be his first stop," Jake said. "But I'll tell ya, Sheriff, I don't think Steve did it."

"Well, we haven't got much to go on, but I do know Allison's reputation." Barnett took a sip from his coffee mug. "I've got an unmarked car up by Edgar's – the Allison kid has been there all day, and his car is in the driveway at home. We'll know if he takes off."

Jake got a slight look of excitement in his eyes. "It's show time. Kelly is getting in his car."

Shawn didn't notice Jake or the Sheriff on the other side of the park as he drove up Main Street. Nor was he aware of being watched when he parked in front of Edgar's and briskly walked inside. He hustled past the car where Richard seemed to be deeply involved with an electrical problem; he waved. "Hello Richard."

"Hi, Shawny. Steve's out back by the Chevy... I think." Richard didn't stop working.

Steve leaned against the fender of the old car, folded his arms across his chest, and grinned. Shawn stared at the lit cigarette Steve was holding. "Got another one of those?"

Steve pulled a cigarette from the pack in his shirt pocket and handed it to Shawn. "Man, you're as nervous as a whore in church." It wasn't difficult for Steve to detect Shawn's uneasiness. "What? Are you all worried about tonight?"

Shawn lit the cigarette, shaking his head. "No. But there's..." He stopped abruptly and looked over his shoulder toward Richard, still engrossed in the maze of wires, gripped Steve's arm firmly and pushed him around the corner, out of the mechanic's sight. "There's something I've got to ask you, and as my best friend, you need to tell me the truth. Did you... did you hurt Sara and take her money Thursday night?"

Steve was usually calm in the face of confrontation. He inherited his cool demeanor from his Dad, who rarely ever got flustered over anything. But at that moment, a bit of anger seeped out. His grin faded to a frown. "Are you out of your mind? You think I had anything to do with that?"

"No, Steve. I don't want to believe it for a minute... but Jake came asking questions this afternoon. They think you could've done it 'cause you were at the bank and saw Sara get a bunch of cash."

Steve's anger turned to a look of fear. "No way! I ain't gonna chase down some old lady and snatch her purse -- *no way.*"

Shawn put a gentle hand on his friend's shoulder. "No matter what they say, I'll be here to stick up for ya – *no matter what.*"

"I may have gotten into a lot of trouble for stuff I didn't do before…" Steve's eyes started to water. "…But they're not gonna pin this one on me."

"Don't worry. I won't let them," Shawn said. "And maybe you shouldn't come with me tonight. They'll probably be watching you."

Steve's eyes widened. "Well that explains why that county cop has been sitting across the street at the drive-in all afternoon."

Shawn chuckled. "Yeah, they probably think you're gonna run off to Mexico with all that money."

Steve was still a little tense, but a hint of a smile crept across his face. "Just how much was I s'pose to have gotten?"

Just the way Steve asked that question, Shawn felt reassured that he was innocent. "A hundred and fifty bucks."

"Oooooo! That much would get me to... let's see... Nebraska?"

They both laughed, and then Shawn turned serious again. "I'm gonna wait 'til dark. I'll get in somehow. I'll call you afterwards, okay?"

"Okay." Steve was disappointed that he wouldn't get in on the library caper. "Take it easy." He gave a soft jab at Shawn's chest. Shawn returned the same gesture, turned and walked back through the garage to his car.

Shawn had done exactly what the lawmen expected he would do; there wasn't any reason to follow him. Surveillance of Steve Allison, though, would continue.

CHAPTER 6

A dome of hazy white brightened the dark night sky off in the direction of the ball field. Not a single car had passed by on the dimly lit back street during the twenty minutes Shawn sat slouched in the driver's seat, windows open, lights and motor off. The crack of a bat occasionally erupted the distant crowd into screaming cheers. "Must be a good game," he thought.

His choice of nights for the mission turned out perfect; in a small town, a baseball tournament was a big event. Every man, woman and child for miles around would be there, lost in the excitement of competition between rival teams, too busy watching the play-by-play action to notice any other lesser activity. Extra police protection was on hand in Westland that night too, but Shawn had already seen the County squad cars – as well as Jake's – parked in strategic positions around the spectator area perimeter, their intimidating presence intended to ensure the crowd's good behavior.

He shivered with a touch of fear. Shawn knew that what he was about to do marked him as a criminal, yet, the danger, the risk, excited him like he'd never experienced before. A boy, looked upon by the whole town as the perfect son, a scholar, a squeaky-clean element of the community, was about to commit a crime. But to him, it seemed a justifiable act, and one he was certain could go undetected. No one had seen him parked on that street, and it seemed quite unlikely there would be any more traffic there, at least until after the ball game, and by then he'd be long gone.

His left hand reached for the door handle; it shook with a nervous quiver. One last time he checked his shirt pocket to make sure the penlight was there, and then gave the door handle a quick, deliberate tug. Seconds later he stood concealed in the shadows of trees behind the library, armed with the jack handle from the Mustang, a penlight, and the desire for this to be over.

With every cautious and precise step, he made his way to the edge of the trees, stopped, and stood as still as a statue, holding his breath, listening and watching for any sign of someone nearby. Nothing. Before him lay twenty feet of barely maintained lawn and the dirt pathway, permanently worn into the grass by sneakers and bicycle tires... and the library's back wall.

Dating back to the very early days of settlement, the red brick single story structure, with part of the basement exposed above ground, endured as one of the city's heirlooms. It had been the Town Marshall's Office and jail in those days, and the steel cell bars still remained encased in the inner walls of the lower level. Shawn thought about the irony – he was attempting to break *into* a jail.

Shawn stared up at the planned entry point – a window much too high for him to reach. He surveyed other possible options, but any other reachable windows were too well lit by the streetlights. He couldn't afford that risk.

A loud whisper pierced through the shadows. "HEY! How do ya think you're gonna get up there, hot shot?"

Shawn nearly jumped out of his skin. He turned and saw the soft moonlight reflecting off Steve's sandy blonde hair. "JEEZ! You scared the crap outa me," he whispered. "And what the hell are you doin' here?" Although he had come with the confidence to accomplish the mission alone, Shawn was elated to know Steve was there with him.

"Oh... I really wanted to go to the lake with my best buddy... but there was this library in the way... so here I am."

Shawn giggled. "What about the cops watching you?"

"Well, Dad was asleep in his recliner. I left him a note... and I guarantee *no one* saw me sneak out through my bedroom window. By the way -- is my sleeping bag still in your trunk?"

"Yup."

"Good. It might get chilly tonight. Now, I believe we have a library to break into?"

Steve's coolness with the situation acted like a bottle of Pepto Bismol on Shawn's anxiety. It remained one of the countless reasons why he liked Steve so much.

Steve knelt down next to the wall beneath the window. "Now get up on my shoulders and let's do this like we planned." Shawn kept his balance with one hand on the brick wall as Steve cautiously rose. He was glad that the shoulders he was standing on were attached to a strong, muscular body, and that body was nearly six feet tall.

Shawn wedged the jack handle under the window frame and pried upward. The screws holding the latch pulled out of the deteriorating wood sill; the window opened easily. He dropped the tool to the ground, pulled himself up, and tumbled awkwardly through the window, onto the library floor. He lay there for a few seconds, listening for any other sounds; Shawn knew there was no one in the building, but paranoia had set in. Scanning the spooky darkness, he gathered his wits, stood, and leaned with his head out the open window. He could barely see Steve in the shadows below. "I'll be back in a few minutes."

Steve picked up the tire iron and stared up at the dark, open window, anxiously waiting for his partner-in-crime to reappear.

The candlepower of the tiny penlight was minimal, but adequate for Shawn to find his way through the familiar layout. The librarian's desk sat across the room, near the front entrance, a distance that now seemed the length of a football field, and each step produced an eerie floorboard squeak that Shawn thought would surely be heard throughout the entire universe. He gingerly pulled back the chair, sat down, and opened the top center drawer. The small halo of light revealed no more than pencils, paper clips, a half-dozen three-by-five cards, and a pair of scissors. Top drawer, right side. A stapler and a note pad with a bunch of names and dates -- probably an overdue book list. More three-by-five cards. Next drawer down. Blank typing paper.

"Wait a minute," he thought. "Sara is left-handed." Top drawer, *left* side. The dim light fell upon a small, leather-bound notebook; the edges of several twenty-dollar bills sandwiched between the pages stuck out. Shawn opened the cover and read the simple contents of the first page:

NAME OF DEPOSITOR: Sara Fremont
ACCOUNT NUMBER: 384-2196

He pulled out the cash and counted one hundred forty dollars.

"This proves Steve didn't steal Sara's money," he said under his breath. He quickly replaced the bills in the book and started to stuff it into his pocket, but then he realized he wouldn't be able to explain where or how he discovered it. It would have to stay right there for someone else to find. He was so excited over this discovery, he almost forgot to continue the search. He slipped the bankbook back to its original spot, and then his fingers fell on the purpose for being there. He lifted the wedge-shaped object out of the drawer; it seemed heavier than he expected -- a pound or more. Even in the dim light, its brilliant sheen paralyzed his senses. A peculiar energy shot through his body as if he were grasping a lightning bolt. Drawn by some mysterious power, he held it, just staring at the luster, wondering if he had interfered with something he shouldn't. Was this what Sara had been referring to? Or was it really the cash?

A loud click reverberated through the quiet room, startling Shawn into realizing he was not alone. He gasped a quick gulp of air and froze. The front door clunked softly as it closed. Someone was definitely in the building with him, but he didn't feel the urge to linger long enough to learn who had entered. It would only be a matter of seconds until the intruder came through the second set of doors and into the room. He could feel his heart pounding like a bass drum in a marching band as he ran across the room to the open window. "Steve! Catch! Somebody's coming! I'm gonna jump. Get the hell outa here!"

Not knowing exactly what he was supposed to catch, Steve stepped back and let the object fall to the ground. Nor did he hear the part about someone else in the building. Shawn's hasty actions and the leap from ten feet above was nothing more than a blur in the darkness. He landed with a thud, but managed to stay on his feet. "You got it? Let's go!" Panic-stricken, Shawn disappeared into the trees.

A large ring of light fell on the grass around Steve, spotlighting him like the player on a stage, and making the metallic wedge quite visible. He grabbed it. "Cool." That instant he realized the light was coming from above and not from Shawn. He looked back up at the window -- a bright flashlight was shining directly into his eyes. He froze momentarily, then sprang to his feet and sprinted to the shadows where Shawn had vanished a few seconds before.

Shawn was behind the wheel with the motor running by the time Steve reached for the passenger side door handle. A clumsy six-week-old puppy could have made a more graceful landing. He sprawled across the seat with one foot on the dash and the other out the window, his head pressed into Shawn's right side.

The Mustang's dual exhaust growled as Shawn unleashed the horsepower and sped down the street, out of town and toward the lake. Steve gathered himself into a normal sitting position and calmly looked over at the pilot. "Well... that was fun. Got anything to eat? I'm starved."

Shawn was too nervous to say much of anything during the rest of the trip to the lake. He could hardly break his thoughts of the other intruder long enough to tell Steve about the cooler full of sodas and hot dogs in the trunk.

The parking lot at the lake was deserted. Usually by 9:30 on a Saturday night there would be a bonfire lighting the beach, and no less than ten or twenty of their schoolmates having a good time. It seemed odd to be there without a transistor radio blaring out the top forty, the smell of smoke in the air, and a few moonlight swimmers splashing in the lake. The silence was almost eerie.

Of course. Double-header baseball was part of it -- but then Shawn remembered the primary reason for the vacant beach on this night: Jamie Johnson's graduation party was probably in full swing, and holding the position of the most popular girl in school, she had, no doubt, drawn quite a crowd. Shawn and Steve had been invited, but now the serenity of the lake had won their interest, and now it didn't seem so strange that they were there all alone.

Steve gathered some half-burned logs and branches left over from previous campfires while Shawn sat on the sandy beach. Deep in thought, he gazed out across the mesmerizing reflection of a full moon on the mirror-like lake surface. He breathed in the fresh forest scents floating on the still night air.

Each time he came here, Shawn was reminded of the stories his father had told him about the valley. Not far from that very spot, his grandfather's water-driven sawmill once stood. Logs cut from the timber of these hills were spread out to dry, then sawed into lumber. Horse-drawn wagonloads of the finished product were hauled to Westland to be sold to the surrounding settlers for their houses, barns and sheds.

Hidden away, off the beaten path, the two-hundred-acre Jasper Valley Lake was the product of a flood control project built in the late 1950's. The earthen dam stretched two hundred yards across the valley, flanked by steep, timber-laden hills. The valley floor had once been rich farm and pasture land with a gurgling stream winding through it, fed by dozens of artesian springs. But with each waning winter season, the otherwise serene creek became an enraged, gushing nightmare with the melting snow and ice accumulated on the surrounding bluffs. The floods destroyed anything and everything in their path, and swept it away without mercy. Now it all lay deep beneath the surface of this calm and peaceful body of water, no longer to be a springtime threat to man or wildlife. The lake had become a haven to ducks and geese, beavers, raccoon, and deer, and was abundant with a variety of game fish. The whole area around Jasper Valley Lake was designated a County Park, and had become a popular -- but not yet overrun -- recreational getaway that provided a perfect natural privacy from the rest of the world.

Steve dropped the armful of wood next to the fire ring; he could sense Shawn's tension. There was no doubt in his mind that Shawn was still unaware of his exposure to the unknown person at the library; Shawn hadn't yet mentioned any knowledge of it, and it would only intensify the tension if he did know. He huddled next to Shawn and began scratching circles and lines in the sand with a stick.

After a few minutes of silence, Steve spoke. "Hey, you got that thing you went after."

Shawn just nodded.

"And the place didn't blow up." Steve pulled out a pack of Marlboros, offered one to Shawn, and lit one himself. Shawn just held the unlit cigarette between his lips.

"You worried about Sara?" Steve asked.

Shawn shrugged his shoulders. "Yeah, I guess... but I'm worried about you, too."

"Me? Why are you worried about me?"

"Because I think I made a big mistake tonight."

"What d'ya mean? By taking that thing from the library?"

"No... by *not* taking something else."

"What?"

"I found the money in Sara's desk."

Steve abruptly stopped the sand etching. "It was there?"

"Yeah, but I put it back in the drawer. We'd never be able to explain how we found it."

"I see your point," Steve said, and resumed drawing in the sand.

"It would have cleared you, and now I'm not so sure that isn't what Sara meant by... *it.*" He lit his cigarette.

"Naw," Steve said, trying to reassure Shawn's confidence. "You thought from the start it was that thing, and you did right by putting the money back."

"Yeah, I hope you're right. Somebody will find it sooner or later, and then they'll know you didn't take it."

"Well," Steve said, trying to change the mood to a more cheerful one. "We're here safe and sound and we've got the beach to ourselves. What could be better? Now let's get this fire goin'. I'm hungry. How 'bout you?"

Shawn felt a bit more relaxed, now that Steve hadn't made a fuss about the failure to exonerate him. "Yeah, guess you're right." He stood up and gave Steve a playful shove. "Get the fire started and I'll get the cooler."

Within minutes a small crackling fire lit up the beach; the smell of smoke and the aroma of roasting hot dogs overpowered the wild valley scents. An hour earlier they had considered themselves hardened criminals; now, they were just two kids on the beach enjoying what they liked best.

They sprawled on sleeping bags spread out next to the fire; the full moon faded into a late night haze.

"I'm gonna go for a swim," Steve declared. "Wanna go for a swim?"

Shawn pondered on that for a few seconds. "But we don't have any dry clothes... or even a towel."

"So what. There's no one else around... and it's not like we've never seen each other naked before."

They stripped to nothing by the light of the fire that, by then, was just an occasional flicker of flames from a heap of glowing embers. They sprinted to the water's edge and plunged into the cool lake. Their uninhibited spirit drew them into oblivious rapture; except for this little plot of aquatic playground, the rest of the universe seemed to evaporate into nonexistence.

Making a stealth approach, perhaps expecting to uncover some illicit activity, Jake detected the silhouette of a car, quickly doused his lights, and rolled to a stop, keeping his car concealed in the shadowy darkness. He, too, was surprised to see the park so empty on such a balmy night, but he was already aware of Jamie Johnson's house party so he didn't think too much of it. He could hear the boys splashing and laughing as they took turns dunking each other. He waited in the shadows. After a few minutes, Shawn and Steve waded back onto the beach. They had nearly reached their clothes, cooler, and sleeping bags, resting on the sand next to an almost dead fire. Jake could only make out the silhouettes of the two, but by the car in the parking lot, he knew exactly who they were. He was just as surprised as the boys when his flashlight exposed the two dripping wet bare bodies, frozen in their tracks, unable to distinguish who was holding the blinding light. Jake broke the silence. "Nice night for a swim." To avoid further embarrassment, he pointed the beam at the ground. Knowing the current situation, there was no reason to feel threatened by the boys he knew. Shawn and Steve, on the other hand, were at the peak of intimidation, especially now that they knew the Police Chief stood only six feet away staring at their naked bodies. It was the second time that night Steve had a flashlight blinding his vision, but at least this time he knew who was on the holding end. His stomach was churning, almost certain it had been Jake at the library, and now he was there to make an arrest. But as usual, Steve kept his composure.

The light beam fixed on the cooler. "Whatya got in there?"

"Just *Pepsi* and hot dogs" Shawn blurted out nervously. Jake leaned over to flip open the lid. "Well I'll be damned... thought for sure there'd be some partyin' goin' on down here tonight."

"Nope. No party here!"

"Just us," Steve added for good measure.

Shawn's mind was racing a mile a minute. Why hadn't Jake said anything about the library?

"You guys leaving soon?"

Shawn was able to breathe normally again, but he was still a little jittery. "Ah...we...were planning on sleeping here on the beach overnight...that okay?"

"Well, I guess there ain't nothin' wrong with that... as long as you behave yourselves."

Steve felt a sudden surge of relief; he realized that Jake did not yet know about the library incident. "We will."

"Okay," Jake said, almost like he was disappointed with what he had found. "You guys take care... I'd better head back into town." Jake turned and started walking back to his car. Shawn and Steve exchanged puzzled stares. When Jake was almost to the car, he chuckled under his breath. He didn't know which was more humorous: catching these two skinny-dipping, or how Steve had slipped away from under the nose of the deputy staking out his house. He opened the car door, and then he heard Shawn call out.

"Hey Jake? Any news about Sara?"

"Nope. Nothing since yesterday. But I'll let you know if I hear anything." Jake started the motor and drove away into the darkness.

After they watched the taillights disappear around the curve, the unclothed boys dropped down onto the sleeping bags spread out by the dying fire, poked at the embers with the roasting sticks to revive some flickering flames, and began to laugh about what had just taken place.

****

Jake was thoroughly convinced that if Steve had any intentions of running, and was capable of escaping the watchful eye of the deputy, he would have certainly run farther than the popular Jasper Valley only five miles away. The Chief was embarrassed nearly to the point of shame that he had even suspected Steve of such an act in the first place. A candid inspection of the '59 Impala in the Allison's driveway had produced nothing out of the ordinary, and until the missing purse and money turned up, there was nothing more than circumstantial evidence that might have connected Steve to the mishap. The more he thought about it, Jake realized the possibility seemed remote, at very best. Now he had to convince the sheriff of that.

He maneuvered the Galaxy alongside the unmarked deputy's car so the two driver's windows were adjacent.

"Might as well go home," Jake said to the deputy who maintained the vigil across the street from Allison's house.

The deputy returned a curious glare.

"He ain't in there," Jake said.

"But I saw him go in around suppertime," the deputy returned, "and he hasn't left. Of course he's in there."

"He's down at the lake with the Kelly boy. I just came from there."

****

The warmth of the morning sun rising over the tree line, high above the shimmering lake surface, awakened Mother Nature's two guests on the beach. They had both slept soundly in the stillness of the cool night air. The last remaining traces of a listless fog drifting just above the water slowly diminished, revealing two fishermen in a small rowboat on the far side of the lake. A brood of eight ducklings lined up behind the hen paddled leisurely along the shoreline past the beach.

They popped open the last two cans of *Pepsi* from the cooler. Shawn scratched his belly. Steve stretched and yawned.

"What is that thing, anyway?" Steve asked.

Shawn was not yet very well educated about the artifact or its significance. "All I know is that Sara found it in the church over fifty years ago. A professor at Luther College encouraged her to investigate its origin, and she's been deeply engaged in its research."

He had noticed her intense interest in the object many times during the past couple of years; he had witnessed Sara pouring over a countless number of publications and making notes as she went along. But to his knowledge, Shawn wasn't aware of any great break-through in discovery, nor had he ever noticed any jubilation on her part to indicate even a trace of success. Now he felt compelled to protect the object of Sara's interest until she could return to it.

"I don't know exactly what it is, but I got this weird sensation last night when I picked it up."

"What kind of sensation?" Steve asked.

"Can't explain it, really. Like it was trying to communicate with me… or something."

"D'ya think someone else is really tryin' to steal it?"

"It's possible." Shawn knew there must be some urgency, or Sara wouldn't have made it the priority at a life-threatening moment. It almost seemed evident that she knew someone else wanted the artifact, but whom? And why had they resorted to violence to get it from her?

Steve wasn't so concerned about the significance of the object, as he was of the unknown invader at the library who saw him carrying it away. If the mystery person was in fact there to snatch the artifact, that would put Steve at risk. He didn't want to cause Shawn any more distress, and concluded there was no reason to compound the problem by informing Shawn that he had been seen -- unless it became absolutely necessary.

****

Late that afternoon, with the weekend winding down, Shawn and Steve settled in the Kelly living room watching a baseball game on television; Hank Aaron slugged in yet another home-run.

The Westland baseball tournament was history. Droves of players and fans were gathered at the Bowling Alley -- winners celebrating, and losers drowning their sorrows of defeat.

And the mysterious artifact was safely tucked away under the driver's seat of the Mustang.

Don Kelly arose from his chair, breaking away from a stack of paperwork as a knock at the side door off the kitchen disrupted his concentration. It was Jake.

The sight of the Police Chief standing in the doorway reinstated a level of paranoia in the living room. At least they were fully clothed now, but the tension was still as thick as window putty. Shawn and Steve exchanged worried glances; surely Jake had discovered the library burglary, and now they would have to face the humiliation in the presence of Shawn's father. Or, maybe Jake was only there to report his observations at the lake to Don; that wouldn't be so bad, but either way, Shawn stood the chance of suffering some sort of embarrassment. They could hear Jake and Don talking in the kitchen, their voices masked by the TV noise. Then a louder and more distinct "Shawn?" called out.

Shawn slowly stood and reluctantly made his way to the kitchen, as if he were taking his last steps to an execution chamber. Steve wasn't about to let his best friend answer the confrontation alone; he followed.

They entered the kitchen and stood across the table from Don and Jake. The tension in that room seemed to be of a different nature; Don's eyes drooped with sadness, and Jake didn't show any signs of aggression.

"I'm afraid I have some bad news," Jake began. "Sara passed away at 2:15 this afternoon."

Devastation poured from Shawn's face. The redness of his expected embarrassment drained, his forehead and cheeks fading to a ghostly pale. Steve forgot about the trouble he was possibly in; it didn't seem important now. He put a hand on Shawn's shoulder and gazed into his watery eyes; he, like almost everyone, understood Shawn's fondness of the gray-haired, pixy-faced Sara Fremont.

Shawn had never experienced the loss of someone close. He barely remembered any of his grandparents, and he was only seven when Grandpa Kelly had died -- too young and resilient for the bereavement to cause lasting pain. But this was now, and there was no escaping the reality of the words Jake had spoken. He felt the tears trickling down his cheeks; without saying a word he turned away from the others and ran up the stairs to his bedroom where he belly-flopped onto the unmade bed, burying his face in the pillow.

Don turned to escort Jake out to his car. Halfway out the door, he paused and turned back toward Steve.

"Talk to him," he said in a concerned tone. "I think he needs a friend right now."

Steve tried to pick the proper words to say to Shawn as he climbed the steps. He sat on the bed, and with a firm but gentle hand he rubbed his sobbing friend's back. "It's gonna be okay, buddy... everything's gonna be okay."

CHAPTER 7

Monday morning began a day filled with more surprises. Several events were destined to change the course of history in Westland, as well as the lives of a few of its inhabitants.

Steve had been at his Dad's shop only a half hour when Andy Kelly appeared at the back door where Steve was toting trash to the barrels outside. His wrinkled, faded, shabby clothing looked as though they had been slept in, and the droopy bags under his eyes suggested he might not have slept at all. Skinny as a rail, his body showed the years of uncontrollable boozing, and it was Steve's guess that Andy's breakfast had been a shot and a beer.

He didn't know Andy very well, and thought it seemed a little peculiar when Andy approached as if to engage in conversation. Steve sensed Andy's uneasiness; Andy stared at him for a few moments, shifted his weight from one foot to the other, and nervously scanned the area to see that no one else was near.

"I know it was you at the library Saturday night," Andy said in a low, guarded voice.

Steve just listened; his brain squirmed like a frog in the hand of a nine-year-old.

"I'll go to the cops, ya know. I saw you jump out the window."

Steve didn't answer. Now he didn't have to wonder any more about who had been shining the light in his eyes from the library window.

"I saw you run off with that thing from Sara's desk."

Steve still said nothing; arguing seemed pointless.

"But I won't tell the cops it was you that broke in, if you give me that thing you took."

"I don't have it," Steve said.

"Oh, but I think you know where it is," Andy said with a sneer.

"No. I don't," Steve lied.

"I'll be back Wednesday to pick it up," Andy demanded. "Have it here for me, and the cops will never know."

"Are you trying to bribe me?"

"*Bribe* is such an ugly idea. Let's call it an *incentive.*"

Steve stood silent. Andy turned to leave. He had been brief and to the point and he was offering no options. He paused, turned to Steve and sternly said once more, "Wednesday morning," and then he disappeared around the corner of the building.

By his description of the event, Andy seemed convinced that it had been Steve acting alone, entering the library, taking the piece, and making good his escape. He had not mentioned any knowledge of Shawn's presence. It was just like Steve's luck: always in the wrong place at the wrong time, and now this pathetic shred of humanity was threatening him with blackmail.

Steve didn't hesitate to get to the phone.

"Shawn. Meet me for lunch at the drive-in. Twelve o'clock sharp. You ain't gonna believe what just happened."

"What? What happened?"

"Can't talk now... to many ears."

"Okay. See ya at noon."

****

The drive-in was the perfect place for a quick burger and a long talk at one of the outdoor picnic tables in the back. Shawn arrived ten minutes early; his curiosity had shifted into high gear.

Steve had been right -- Shawn found it hard to believe that his own uncle had turned the library incident into an episode of the *Keystone Cops*. And even more absurd was his extortion attempt. It just didn't make any sense -- the situation was getting crazier by the minute.

"Why would Andy want that thing? And how did he know it was there?" Steve threw Shawn a puzzling look.

"Andy certainly isn't after the artifact for scientific purposes," Shawn pondered. He knew there had to be some other motivation prompting Andy's actions. "It's anybody's guess how Andy has become involved."

"Well, we've got until Wednesday morning," Steve said. "I'll be in big trouble if Andy goes to the cops."

"Don't worry 'bout that," Shawn assured. "I'll think of something."

"Maybe we should just give it to him," Steve suggested.

"No way. I'm not going to just hand it over to him, or to anyone else."

"Then we'd better find a better place to hide it."

"Got any suggestions?"

Steve dove into deep thought, staring across the highway to the garage. "How about the old Chevy?"

"Yeah. Nobody would ever look there," Shawn agreed. "Tonight... we'll do it tonight."

****

Andy Kelly sat in his dreary little apartment above the hardware store with the phone receiver pressed to his ear, envisioning giant dollar signs parading across the living room floor. "I'll have it by Wednesday noon," he boasted.

"Excellent," came the reply. "I knew I could count on you."

"But you'll have to come here to get it."

"I can do that."

"Meet me in the High School parking lot... *with the cash*... at two o'clock."

****

Westland's City Council usually met the first Monday of each month, but Sara Fremont's untimely death had created the opening for a librarian; it warranted a special meeting to be called. All the available teachers of the school system had been contacted by the City Clerk's Office, but none of them were willing to make a commitment. Tax dollars maintained the operation of the library facility, and it wasn't fair to deprive the public of its service to the community. The council was faced with the need of at least a temporary solution.

Shawn Kelly's name was brought to the table; he was eighteen years old, a High School graduate, and no other person in Westland had spent more time there, or was more familiar with the library. He wasn't the last choice, by any means, but he was the best one. Unanimously, Shawn was declared the primary candidate to fill the job, and an offer would be extended to him the very next day.

****

While the aldermen conducted their meeting at City Hall, the tires of Jake's new squad car crunched across the graveled Bowling Alley parking lot. His thoughts drifted from a work routine; Monday nights usually proved mundane, and this was no exception. The town was behaving quite nicely after the weekend baseball tournament; Jake was glad it was over.

Only a dozen cars nosed up to the Bowling Alley walls, like a litter of piglets to a sow's belly at feeding time. Jake recognized most of them as belonging to regular patrons of the popular watering hole, and like any other Monday night, the activity level seemed to be rather subdued. Another hour of patrolling, making himself visible on the streets, and he could go home.

As his car slowly idled past the row of vehicles, something out of the ordinary caught his eye; it deserved a second look. The side mirror on a maroon Oldsmobile appeared to be broken off at the base and dangled by the remote control cable. Jake's instincts demanded he make a closer inspection. With flashlight in hand he approached the Oldsmobile and fixed the beam on the broken mirror.

His eyes widened. A lump formed in his throat. Jake quickly returned to his car and grabbed the radio microphone.

"Car 52 to headquarters," he spoke.

"Go ahead Jake," the County dispatcher responded.

"Is the Sheriff available tonight?" Jake asked, a tone of urgency painting his voice.

"He's right here in the office."

A few seconds later Sheriff Barnett's voice came through the radio speaker. "What do ya need, Jake?"

Jake keyed the mic. "There's something you need to see here, Sheriff."

"What is it?"

"I'd rather not say on the air. Can you get over here right away?"

"I'll be there in fifteen minutes. Where are you?"

"The Bowling Alley parking lot."

Barnett's experience had taught him to read voices on the radio; Jake's urgent tone convinced him to waste as little time as possible. He arrived at the parking lot ten minutes later.

"Take a look at this, Sheriff," Jake said. He pointed Barnett toward the Oldsmobile.

The Sheriff stared at the broken mirror. "What? You drug me out here to show me a broken mirror?"

"Look closer," Jake said, and held his flashlight beam on the jagged edge of the broken metal. A tiny shred of fabric clung to it.

Barnett stooped down, his face inches from the snag. He looked back up at Jake, still not quite sure what Jake was implying.

"The color of the cloth," Jake said. "It's the same color as the dress Sara Fremont was wearing last Thursday night."

"Are you sure?"

"Positive," Jake answered. "I helped put her on the stretcher."

Barnett went to his car; seconds later he returned with a small clear plastic bag, carefully pulled the fabric from the broken mirror and stuffed it into the bag.

It was as if Sara had left her signature.

They both knew who owned the Oldsmobile. It always seemed more difficult to carry out the unbiased expectations of a law enforcement officer when situations like this occurred, but it was their duty as servants of the community to continue the investigation. An unpleasant arrest was imminent.

****

Shawn and Steve were busy that night too. The old Chevy sat in the back stall at Edgar's, hood up, trunk lid and both doors open. To anyone passing by and peering through the windows, it would appear as the usual nightly routine of two novice mechanics pursuing a dream that few believed would ever reach reality. All critics, though, had by then accepted the boys' persistence, and no one questioned why the light at Edgar's burned into the late night hours. Jake would pull up to the front now and then, but when he realized it was Steve and Shawn tinkering inside, he'd just wave and drive off. That old blue Chevy provided an element of privacy.

And privacy was what Shawn and Steve needed most right then; with her last spoken words, Sara had entrusted them with a mysterious secret that neither of them understood. The strange artifact represented danger; they both knew it. Someone else wanted it, but Shawn's loyalty to dear, departed Sara remained rigid. It represented a certain unknown cloak-and-dagger thrill, too; that was the most intriguing part of it to Shawn, and Steve seemed to be growing more captivated by the minute.

"I found the perfect spot," Steve whispered. He crawled out the passenger side door and stood, his face smudged with ten-year-old dust. "Under the dash… behind the glove box."

"Sounds good to me," Shawn replied. "I'll get it out of my car."

The same weird sensation he'd felt the night at the library penetrated deep into him again as his hand found the piece under the Mustang seat. He brought it out into the light, staring intensely at the peculiar etchings on the wedge-shaped object, and wondered if Sara had ever experienced the curious sensation. He couldn't recall ever seeing Sara holding it, or even touching it. All he could remember was her probing at it and pushing it around the desk with a pencil.

He carried it to the old Chevy as if it were a priceless piece of crystal and held it out to Steve.

"Hold it, Steve, and tell me if you feel anything strange," Shawn said.

Steve's first thought was that Shawn meant strange to the touch, and didn't expect anything else. He took the artifact in one hand and began rubbing it gently with the other. Almost immediately his movement stopped, as if he had been instantly frozen. His eyes narrowed and his cheeks tightened. One eyebrow raised. He tried to speak. "What--?"

Shawn knew right away, by the expression on Steve's face, that he felt the energy transmitting from the artifact.

"What do you think it is?" Steve whispered.

"I don't know," Shawn answered. "Kinda wild, ain't it?"

Steve quickly placed it on the roof of the old car. "Think it's dangerous?"

"No," Shawn replied. "I don't think so. Feels more like…" He paused in thought. "I don't know."

They stared at the object on the roof for a long while, puzzled by their experience. Neither could attach an explanation to it, but both knew they were viewing something quite extraordinary.

"We can't let anyone else get it," Shawn said. "Not until we find out what it is."

"That could take forever," Steve mumbled.

"Then, we'll keep it forever."

Steve glanced at the clock above the office door. "It's getting late. Let's hide this thing and call it a night."

"Yeah," Shawn agreed. "Get a light so I can see under the dash." He plucked the artifact off the roof and laid it on the seat cushion. Steve plugged in a work light while Shawn positioned himself on the floorboard beneath the dash, ready to dispose of the artifact to its prescribed hiding place behind the glove box. As Steve passed the light through the open car door to Shawn, it cast a flood of illumination onto the seat and the metallic wedge. Tiny threads of light, like multi-colored, miniature search beacons reflected from the artifact, projecting dozens of spots and lines onto the car's headliner.

"Shawn! Look at this." Steve's voice exploded with excitement.

"I see it," Shawn responded with an equal portion of exhilaration.

Puzzled by the inconsistent lines and symbols projected onto the car ceiling, they studied the pattern, but it seemed so incomplete, somehow, even though they didn't know exactly what they were viewing. Comparing the projected images to the markings on the wedge, there was a significant difference -- the etchings on the metallic surface didn't necessarily correspond with the reflections.

"Well this changes everything," Shawn said.

"D'ya s'pose Sara knew about this?"

"Hard to say, but I bet she didn't."

"What are we gonna do about your Uncle?"

"I'll talk to him before Wednesday. Maybe I can call off the wolves."

CHAPTER 8

"Hello," Shawn mumbled.

The phone rang again.

"Hello." Shawn realized his eyes weren't open and that he was answering a non-existent receiver in his clenched fist pressed against his cheek. He consciously listened for another ring, and when it sounded again he opened his eyes just enough to detect daylight.

The persistent ringing didn't stop.

"Okay, okay, I'm coming," he mumbled, fully expecting to hear his father's lecture about staying up too late again. Stumbling down the stairs, he cleared his throat, preparing himself to sound wide-awake.

"Hello," he answered, as if he'd been up for hours.

"Hi… Shawn?" came the unexpected feminine voice.

"Yes?"

"This is Melanie at the City Clerk's Office…"

Shawn listened to the librarian job proposal, eagerly wanting to accept without further consideration.

"Sure… I'll talk to my Dad about it," he replied, "and I'll let you know later today."

It seemed like the perfect opportunity; all traces of the Saturday night visit to the library could be wiped clean. The broken window latch could be repaired before anyone else noticed it, and most importantly, Shawn could get Steve off the hook, once and for all, by rediscovering the bankbook and cash that Sara had left behind. He'd report it to Jake immediately; Steve would be exonerated of all suspicion. Perfect. It was like trumpets blaring a fanfare and a voice like that of God Himself announcing Steve's innocence.

****

With all the finesse of a bull moose in a minefield, Shawn burst into his father's office at the lumberyard.

"Dad! Guess what!"

Don Kelly glanced at Shawn, then the clock, and fixed one of those do-you-know-what-time-it-is? glares into Shawn's eyes.

"Sorry I'm late, but I got a phone call this morning from the City Clerk's office." Too much excitement kept him from waiting for his father's response. "They offered me a job at the library."

Don settled back into his chair and folded his arms across his chest. He said nothing, but Shawn knew his expression was that of disappointment.

"Don't worry, Dad. I'll still work here too. The library is just nights… and it's only temporary."

"So when do you start?" Don asked.

"They want me to pick up the keys this afternoon, and I'll start tonight."

****

After a day at the lumberyard that seemed like it would never end, Shawn slipped the key into the lock and slowly pulled the library front door open. It was a feeling of exhilaration; he was about to begin a job that wouldn't seem like work at all. A flip of the light switch revealed the familiar room – a room where he had spent countless hours, but now it levied a different kind of atmosphere. Sara was not there.

He walked across the squeaky floor toward the window, glancing down each isle of bookshelves, as if expecting to see Sara on her tiptoes atop the stepstool trying to reach the top shelf, like she often did. The stool was there, but Sara wasn't.

Tears once again threatened. Shawn stopped his pace toward the window and stood motionless in the silence. He thought about all the good times he and Sara had spent there; he thought about his academic success, that Sara had helped him to achieve; he thought about his failure to arrive there early enough on Thursday night.

Like the annoying buzz of an alarm clock, the sound of the front door opening jarred Shawn from his pensive state. He wasn't ready to meet the public just yet.

"Shawn?" his father's voice echoed.

In a moment of urgency, Shawn stared at the window latch, anticipating the sight of obvious damage that he wanted no one to see, but it had already been repaired. Relieved, but puzzled, he turned to greet his father. "Checkin' up on me already?" he said, stepping toward the desk.

"No," Don said.

Shawn pulled back the chair and sat down at the desk.

"Just wanted to let you know," Don continued, "I might not be home when you get there."

"Why?" Shawn pulled open the desk drawer. It would be a good time to find the bankbook and money.

"I have to go to the Sheriff's Office."

Shawn stared into the empty drawer. The money was not there. It wasn't in any drawer.

Don noticed the worried look on his face as Shawn opened one drawer after another. "What's wrong? Lose something?"

"Um... no... it's nothing," Shawn stuttered. "Why do you have to go to the Sheriff's Office?"

"Andy's been arrested."

"Drunk driving? Again?" Shawn was preoccupied with the oddities of the repaired window latch and the vanished money.

"Worse than that. Hit and run."

"Really! What happened?"

Don looked into his son's eyes, fearful of the reaction that might come. "Sara," he said softly.

Shawn gasped. His eyes widened, and then narrowed to just slits. A thousand images raced through his mind, but none of them clearly satisfied the mystery.

"*Uncle* Andy?" he finally asked.

"They found a shred of Sara's dress on his car. Kind of looks like he did it."

Shawn said nothing. He just stared off into the distance.

"I have to go," Don said. "Are you gonna be okay?"

"Yeah, I'll be fine. Steve's coming over later," Shawn muttered, watching his father head for the front door.

Now things were *really* getting strange. Shawn knew Andy was no model citizen, but could he really be responsible for Sara's death? And if it really was Andy who caught him there Saturday night, he must have lifted the cash. But that would be hard to prove, if not impossible. Shawn couldn't report to Jake that he knew the money was in the desk drawer -- that would implicate him in a burglary that no one else knew had taken place. No one except one other person – Andy. But would Andy really say anything? He didn't have a legitimate reason for entering the library that night, either.

Shawn was drawing himself deeper and deeper into a well of deception as he continued to keep the artifact a secret. It appeared that the police were unaware of its existence; if they were informed of it, Shawn feared he would have to turn it over to them, and he couldn't let that happen. No, it was better to just keep it quiet.

Shawn quickly abandoned his feelings of guilt for snooping through Sara's desk. It was *his* desk now, and he knew Sara's research notes were there. He had seen them earlier.

Sara had compiled forty-seven pages of information from dozens of books related to ancient writings, but no mention of the peculiar energy, or the spectacular reflective characteristics. The lack of that information confirmed Shawn's speculations: Sara didn't know, or at least she hadn't noted the knowledge.

Now it was a matter of retracing her steps through all that literature, but this time with some new data. Shawn had his work cut out for him.

On the last page of Sara's notes, the name W. Taylor and a 612 area code phone number was penciled in the margin. He studied the name a few moments, and then recalled the night he had dropped off his term paper for Sara to proof read. She had referred to the gray-haired man sitting at her desk that night as "Professor Taylor."

****

Wednesday morning, a request came from the county jail. Andy needed some clothing picked up from his apartment and brought to him. Shawn was appointed to the errand.

He was somewhat surprised to find Andy's abode in much better condition than he expected. In Shawn's mind, Andy had always been, more or less, a bum, but his dwelling didn't reveal that -- it was neat and respectable. As he emerged from the bedroom where he located the desired apparel, he noticed a note pad on a table by the phone. He couldn't help but see a message written on the pad: the same 612 number as he had found in Sara's research notes, and "$5000--Wed--2:00."

The strange had just become stranger. Some of the puzzle pieces were falling into place: Professor Taylor was offering a reward to Andy for retrieving the artifact. Andy was only acting as a middleman, carrying out the dirty work. Now that he had been arrested and jailed before he could carry out his blackmail threat on Steve, that pressure was off, but that only meant Taylor might still pursue his passion by means of some other unknown menace.

A blast of anger heated Shawn's veins. His own uncle was responsible for Sara's death; Sara's trusted friend had betrayed her; and now, Shawn was delegated to deliver socks and underwear to the villain's accomplice.

One thing was certain, though: *Taylor would never get his hands on the artifact.*

CHAPTER 9

Following the burial ceremony on Friday, Sara's family and friends gathered in the church basement for the usual funeral lunch. Shawn was only seven years old when he had last seen Pastor Fremont; certainly the aged minister wouldn't recognize him as a young adult, but Shawn's family had always been members of this congregation, and maybe the Kelly name would stir some recollections.

After a long wait, Shawn finally got his turn to relay heart-felt sympathy to the Fremonts. Once the conversation was under way, Pastor Fremont recognized Shawn as one of his "flock" -- and one of Sara's dearest friends. She had spoken of Shawn often, and now it seemed as though he was the most important person in the room. The old Pastor soon began sharing his memories of the long-past days when he and his family first came to Westland, and how Sara, as just a tike, made the church her playground. That made for the perfect opportunity for Shawn to inquire about the artifact.

"Oh, sure. I remember that," the old man replied. It seemed to bring back some fond memories for him as well. "She called it her magic rock. But how do you know about that?"

Shawn knew immediately they were discussing the same object. "She told me once that she found it in the attic of this church."

"Yes, she played there often... while I wrote my sermons in my office."

"Has she ever mentioned anything about it to you lately?"

The old man rubbed his chin. "Only that she was looking into its origin, but I don't know if she ever found anything."

"Well, Sara gave it to me, and now I'm continuing her research."

"So that's why you're so curious."

"Yeah, I was hoping you might know something about it."

"No, I don't. But there were more of them -- four or five."

Shawn's eyes widened to the size of a dinner plate. "What happened to 'em?"

"We didn't know what they were, so we just left them there in the attic."

****

Only after making a thorough hunt for the stairway to the attic, which he could not find, he started asking questions. More than ten years earlier, the church had undergone an extensive remodeling. The door at the entrance to the stairwell leading to the attic had been walled over. The attic still existed, but the only access was through a crawl space running the full length of the building above the ceiling from the bell tower. The last person to go up there had been an electrician who ran the new wiring before the project began.

Kelly Lumber had supplied the materials for the facelift, but the only blueprints on file didn't provide any help -- they only showed the areas that were affected by the actual work, which didn't include the attic or the passageway to it. Any other access to the attic didn't seem to exist.

****

Steve kept Shawn company for several nights at the library. He, too, had become intrigued, as together they retraced Sara's prior search through book after book, hoping to find something that might have been missed the first time. But even with the newfound reflecting characteristic, they found nothing to indicate any explanation or significance. Shawn realized the other pieces that Sara's father had mentioned were the missing links, and by the time Sara began her research, the attic door was already blocked. So for her, retrieving them was out of the question. Shawn was feeling frustration.

"Without those other pieces, we aren't gonna find anything."

Steve could tell that thought was quite disappointing to Shawn. "So you're gonna give up? Just like that?"

"No," Shawn renewed his spirit of enthusiasm. "We need to get into the church attic."

"And just what are we gonna tell 'em why we need to get up there?"

"We're not." Shawn eyed Steve with a devious little grin.

"No... Shawn... *no*." Steve wasn't too much in favor of what his buddy was suggesting. "The library was one thing, but I ain't breakin' into no church."

Shawn was quick to respond with a compromising condition. "We don't have to *break* in. Next Sunday, I'll sneak out during the sermon -- like I have to use the bathroom. I'll unlock one of the basement windows. No one will ever notice that. We'll get in through there. Simple."

"Yeah! That's what you said about the last time."

CHAPTER 10

By Sunday, Shawn's mother, Kathy, had returned from her longer-than-originally-planned visit at her brother's home in Missouri. She was tired after the long bus ride from Kansas City, and she was ready to skip the Sunday morning service, but Shawn insisted they attend.

The Kellys occupied a pew at about the center of the church where they usually sat. Shawn immediately began sizing up the layout. He paid particular attention to the overhead, making mental notes of all the dimensions the best he could by estimation. Imagining what would be encountered to reach the otherwise inaccessible room was not easy. The ceiling above the altar dropped down about eight feet from the rest of the arched nave ceiling. The crawl space, then, must be at the very peak of the roof, and the attic floor must be eight feet below it, making what appeared to be the most difficult -- but certainly not insurmountable --obstacle between the bell tower and the attic. He had already taken notice of the trap door directly under the tower as they entered the church, and recognized it by association with similar units Kelly Lumber displayed in their showroom. It was one that supported a ladder that unfolded and extended to the floor when the spring-loaded door was pulled open from below. He made the assumption that there would be a built-in ladder the rest of the way up the tower. Sorting everything out, he thought it might not be so difficult after all.

Richard and Steve Allison sat directly across the center aisle from the Kellys. Steve, too, was simultaneously making the same observations. He knew that night would be the night, when he caught a glimpse of Shawn whispering to his Dad, and then quietly slipped away toward the back of the church. When he returned a few minutes later, he winked at Steve. The key preparation had been completed.

****

It was no wonder that Don retired to the living room couch and drifted off into an afternoon siesta after the wonderfully delicious roast beef dinner with all the trimmings. It was the first home-cooked meal like that he had eaten in nearly three weeks.

But upstairs behind the closed door of Shawn's room, there was no time for a nap. The master plan for that night's mission was taking form. Shawn suggested they have with them a bag to carry out the pieces -- if they found them. A pillowcase would be perfect. It was Steve's idea to take ten feet of nylon rope, in case they needed a means to get down to the attic floor from the crawl space, and back up again. Other than a flashlight with fresh batteries for each of them, these were the only items that should be needed. Later in the evening, they would announce to the rest of the family their intentions to go to Edgar's, where they would be working on the old car. They would push the '56 into the garage, raise the hood, and leave one light on in the back of the building, as to appear they were there to anyone driving by. Once again, not only did they have a plan, they had an alibi.

****

Until that night, the summer had been hot and dry. But now the sky threatened the approach of a thunderstorm. Dark, lightning-filled clouds boiled, pushed by a gusty wind. The distant rumble of thunder was getting closer by the minute; sprinkles of rain dotted the sidewalks.

Shawn parked the Mustang in the empty lot adjacent to Kelly Lumber, four blocks from the church. The streets were nearly deserted, which wasn't unusual for 10:15 on a Sunday night. Frequent flashes from the electrified atmosphere lit up the darkest shadows, and the cultural expressions of the city seemed to dance in the spectacular light show.

Before them loomed the lofty and majestic structure, with its footings implanted solidly in time. Its magnificent multi-colored stained glass windows and the nineteenth century architecture suggested the great importance its builders had placed on their faith. Towering high above any other man-made structures, the steeple seemed to be reaching to the heavens, daring the lightning to come near.

The third window on the south wall of the church was still unlatched, allowing the two treasure hunters to gain access into the main activity hall of the basement. This, too, was a familiar place -- there was no question of the route to reach their destination just below the bell tower.

The looped rope attached to the trap door was just out of reach, making it necessary for Steve to jump up to attain an effective grip. As his body weight pulled the door open, the springs and hinges of the mechanism screeched, and sent shrilling echoes throughout the cavernous, empty church interior. They both froze in terror, and then realized they were alone. Even that sound wouldn't be heard on the outside of the thick-walled structure.

Just as Shawn anticipated, the ladder attached to the inside of the door unfolded and extended to the floor. Pointing his flashlight beam upward into the tower shaft revealed another ladder built into the wall all the way to the top. Equivalent to three stories up, what appeared to be another trap door, closed off the upper end of the vertical passageway. A three-quarter inch thick rope hung through the center of the shaft, and disappeared through the upper door where it continued on up to the huge iron bell above. As they had it calculated, the entry to the crawl space was on the wall adjacent to the one with the ladder, and shouldn't present an impasse in their journey to the attic. Steve led the way up the six-foot square tower. A draft rushing up the shaft produced an eerie whine as the air escaped through the cracks around the upper trap door. Vibrations from the thunder added to the ominous atmosphere within the column. As he neared the upper limits, Steve's flashlight beam found a hinged, three-foot square door held closed by a hasp. It seemed logical this was the opening that would expose the entry into the crawl space. But the latch was rusted; it hadn't been opened in years. Now Steve was aware of why he anticipated the possible need of the pair of pliers tucked into his back pocket. Maneuvering proved tricky as he clutched the flashlight and the ladder rung with one hand, and worked the rusty latch using the pliers with his free hand. All Shawn could do was watch from just below Steve's feet. As the hasp finally broke loose and the small door swung open into the darkness of the crawl space, Steve lost his balance from the sudden movement. With his free hand he grabbed at anything that might catch his fall. That something was the large rope at the center of the tower. His weight on the rope caused its slight downward movement --just enough to roll the bell to one side. "BONG-g-g-g-g" reverberated through the belfry as the pliers ricocheted from wall to wall and dropped to the floor below. Inside the tower shaft, the resonant tone was intense, however, outside, the subdued peal was barely audible midst the howling wind and rolling thunder. But Shawn didn't realize, that instant, that the ringing bell was muted by the weather conditions. "You rang the bell!"

As if to acknowledge the obvious, Steve calmly replied, "No shit, Sherlock!"

Shawn scolded his comrade in a joking tone. "Hey... watch your language, Watson... we're in a church."

They both realized, at that very moment, they had acquired nicknames for each other. No one else would ever know or understand the origin. And the names *did* seem quite appropriate.

Steve crawled through the tiny doorway into the cramped corridor. Shawn was right on his heels. Once inside, they paused in perfect silence trying to detect if the bell had attracted any attention, but the only sounds they could hear were the wind, thunder, and rain falling on the roof only inches from their heads.

On hands and knees, they made their way from rafter to rafter, unable to tell what awaited them at the other end of the long tunnel. An opening, much like the one they came through from the bell tower was there, except this one had no door obstructing their passage. They had predicted fairly accurate dimensions of the layout. The attic floor was about an eight-foot drop from where they were perched. From that vantage point, they scanned the room with their flashlights.

It was empty except for rubble left behind from the remodeling. Apparently, it had been used as a workshop during the project, as piles of sawdust and scraps of wood lay strewn about. One small window on the far wall emitted lightning blue flashes from the intensifying storm.

Steve unwrapped the rope wound around his waist, tied one end to the rafter he was kneeling on, and tossed the other end over the ledge. Like repelling rock climbers, one by one they descended onto the attic floor.

Entangled in a gob of cobwebs and breathing the musty air, they turned slowly, their flashlight beams zigzagging about the unpainted walls and bare wood floor.

"Where do we start?" Steve said quietly.

Shawn's light found a heap of rubble in a corner of the room. "We'll start there... in that corner and work our way around."

They dug through the pile finding nothing more than wood scraps and sawdust. Along the length of the wall, the next corner, another wall, and yet another corner, more of the same.

Shawn kept kicking at the debris; he noticed Steve's light moving farther away toward the corner they had not yet searched, but he continued the scrutiny of the rubble at his feet. He did not notice Steve disappearing down the stairway.

"Sherlock!" he heard Steve call out. He turned to find Steve's light, but it was nowhere in sight.

"Sherlock!" Steve called out again. "I found them!"

"Where are you?" Shawn said, confused with where the voice was coming from.

"The stairway," Steve answered, and pointed his flashlight upward as a beacon for Shawn to follow.

There, on the third step from the bottom, covered with years worth of dust, sat the four pieces, neatly stacked just as they had been left some five decades ago. Steve brushed away the dirt and carefully handed them, one by one, to Shawn. The same strange energy radiated from those four pieces too, and there in the darkness of the attic, the spooky sensation seemed more intense. The four wedge-shaped pieces looked just like the one they already had, and when the wedges were positioned together, they formed a round disc, less one section, like a pie with one slice removed. By that, they determined they had found the complete set. They rejoiced in their success.

Shawn unfurled the cloth bag tucked in his belt and put the pieces into it. "Let's get outa here."

They scaled the eight-foot wall and made their way back through the crawl space. It sounded as if the storm was subsiding. It was just a matter of descending the tower, leaving everything as they had found it, and taking a leisurely four-block walk to the car. Except for accidentally ringing the bell, the plan had worked quite smoothly.

The outside air felt cool and refreshing. The rain had stopped, but lightning still flashed and the thunder crackled in the aftermath of the departing tempest.

"Mission complete," Shawn whispered. He pulled the window shut and rose to his feet beside Steve. They were swollen with pride over their profound accomplishment. But the mission was *not* finished -- they had an unexpected visitor. A dark figure approached from out of the shadows, aiming a bright light into their eyes.

"Oh shit," Steve mumbled in sort of a whine. "Not this again?"

"Hello boys" the proper English voice said. As not to draw any attention, the man turned off the light, allowing Shawn and Steve to see their captor. Even in the dim luminescence from a distant streetlight, Shawn recognized the gray-haired man. It was Professor Taylor. Steve saw what he thought was a pistol pointed at them.

"I can assume you were successful with your quest tonight. There seems to be something in the bag. Now if you would be so kind as to hand it over to me."

Shawn didn't yet realize that Taylor had a gun. "But how did you--"

"I overheard your conversation with Miss Fremont's father at the funeral. I was seated at the next table. I knew it was just a matter of time until you would retrieve the other pieces. I've been watching you all week. I even saw you making your calculations and preparations at the worship service this morning. Now give me the bag, please."

Steve knew there was five or six pounds of dead weight in the bottom of the sack. With no intention of letting go, he swung his strong arm back, and hurtled the bag toward Taylor. A direct hit, right between the eyes. Taylor was more startled than hurt, but it still knocked him off balance. As he fell backwards to the wet ground, two rounds popped from the semi-automatic into the air. Shawn and Steve didn't waste any time to vacate the area, as they were already three strides into a dead run, top speed in four. Shawn wasn't thinking about the possibility of anyone seeing them running down the street at 11:30 at night. His only concern at that moment was to put as much distance between them and that gun-wielding lunatic, as quickly as possible. The Mustang was staged for take-off just four blocks away. At the two-block mark, Steve yelled at Shawn, who was only a couple of strides ahead. "Next time...park the car...a little closer?"

Both doors of the Mustang swung open simultaneously. Shawn had left the key in the ignition so the motor was running almost as soon as he hit the seat. Steve tossed the bag into the rear seat and dove in after it, landing awkwardly with one leg dangling over the backrest of the passenger bucket seat and the other over Shawn's right shoulder. The car's abrupt forward motion caused the passenger's door to slam shut. "Man! I've got to work on these emergency landings."

Shawn thought they would be far ahead of the predator, so he played it cool as he cruised up Main Street, just in case there might be a cop lurking in the shadows. Steve was struggling between the bucket seats to take up his shotgun position next to Shawn. "Sherlock...who the hell was that?"

"*That*, my dear Watson, was the Professor Taylor."

Steve had gathered up all his poise. "Well... didn't sound any bigger than a twenty-two."

Shawn didn't calm down so easily. "I don't care *how big* it was... it was shootin' *bullets... at us!"*

Steve stared at Shawn with a somewhat puzzled look. "I thought he was the guy who was willing to pay big bucks for this stuff."

Shawn had his eyes on the rear view mirror. "Not any more... and if that asshole has been watching us, we'll hafta go somewhere he doesn't know."

They passed the last street light heading out the highway toward the lake road as Shawn saw the image of the black Continental beginning to fill his mirror. "Shit! That's probably him. Hang on!" He knew the Lincoln would eat his Mustang alive on a straight road, but if he could get enough of a jump on him, the 'Stang could easily out-maneuver him on the crooked lake road. At

120, the green horse just wasn't going to get any faster. He had gained a considerable lead on that burst of acceleration, but the black Lincoln wasn't that far behind, and it was starting to close in. It was just a little farther to the lake road turn-off. Hard on the brakes; downshift to third gear; second gear; hard right onto the lake road and airborne over the railroad crossing. Third gear; hard on the brakes again into the first curve to the left; then right. Fourth gear and pour on the gas down the mile-long straight.

"Sherlock! You dumb ass! This is a dead end at the lake. Where ya gonna go from there?"

"Dunno! Maybe we'll have to swim across the lake."

One more S-curve, and then it was only a hundred yards to the beach parking lot. Shawn was hoping Taylor didn't know what was at the end of this road; with a little luck, maybe *he'd* go for a swim. Steve was watching out the rear window as Shawn locked up all four wheels and put the Mustang into a 180 degree spin, coming to rest pointing in the direction they had just come, and ready to make a fleeing escape if necessary. The pursuing headlights suddenly appeared, but the Continental wasn't on the pavement; it plowed through the roadside weeds, bounced violently across the shallow ditch, and slammed head-on into an immense oak tree.

"*Holy shit!*" Shawn eased up to the wreck. A cloud of steam rolled out from under the buckled hood and engulfed the black car. One headlamp was still lit, pointed at the ground. Shawn's lights illuminated the interior of the twisted Lincoln. The driver was slumped over the steering wheel, motionless, and his face, red with blood.

****

Jake came to the door dressed in blue jeans and an unbuttoned plaid shirt. Even Steve was a little excited as he explained the situation. "Bad accident out by the lake... car hit a tree... the guy looks hurt... bad!"

Within thirty seconds, the Chief was in his car, red lights flashing and siren screaming.

CHAPTER 11

The library wasn't a safe place to examine the newfound artifacts. Security was still an issue; there would be less risk of anyone seeing them and asking questions if the continued scrutiny was carried out in the after-hours privacy at Edgar's.

The five wedge-shaped pieces fit together so precisely, no matter what order they were arranged to form the circle. Shawn was sure they must have been crafted by highly skilled hands with the help of a certain amount of technology. There was no rust or corrosion on the material that appeared to be some sort of metal alloy similar to stainless steel, but much lighter weight, and more of a bronze color. The etched and machined markings were of various depths and configurations, and a wide variety of shades of the bronze-like coloration, much brighter than the pieces themselves. The only markings that seemed to be identical on all five pieces were three lines from side to side, arced the opposite of the outer edge. When the pieces were fitted together, the lines matched, end to end, to form the similarity of a perfectly concentric spider's web. All other markings were different on each piece, although some were repeated in various locations.

"We need a better surface to project the reflections onto," Shawn said. "Something dark-colored."

"I'll find a big piece of cardboard… and some black spray paint."

"Yeah! That would work perfect."

As before, the etchings projected an entirely different image on the black overhead screen -- all except the spider web. It was still present in that same pattern; only the arcs appeared as overlapping double lines.

Seemingly harmless, the peculiar sensation of energy remained, and now a bit more intense after the five wedges had been reunited.

"S'pose there's some sort of power source sealed inside them?" Steve pondered, exercising his inclinations.

"Could be," Shawn responded. "Or maybe it's just residual static electricity."

They had no idea if they would ever learn anything of importance from the wedges, but Shawn's determination to continue with Sara's research was stronger than ever. And now there was so much more to work with. But there had to be hundreds of arrangement combinations, and so far, they couldn't come up with one that made any more sense than it had before. Every *pie* arrangement produced just another version of confusing gibberish encompassed in a spider web reflected on a piece of black cardboard. Nothing more.

Clearly obvious, Professor Taylor couldn't be trusted, even though he was the only person who might have a clue. In a hospital bed recovering from the accident, he couldn't pose much of a threat, for the time being. But as of late, Taylor had proved, more than once, that he was capable of fiendish surprises, with or without help. It was just a matter of time until he would strike again. Shawn knew he and Steve stared into the face of danger, but with Taylor, they had no way of predicting his next move, or who might be making it. And it was the best thrill either of them had ever experienced.

"We've gotta stay a step ahead of him," Shawn said, a scheme bubbling in his head.

Steve's keen sense of perception detected another caper brewing. Already, he had been suspected of the original tragedy; twice, he risked his neck to retrieve the mystic artifacts; twice, he had narrowly escaped capture; he had been shot at, chased and threatened with blackmail. Surely, any connection to these strange objects posed likelihood of hazard and more dangerous risks. Steve craved more. He was ready for the excitement.

"So, what are we gonna do next?" Steve asked.

"Maybe there's something in his car," Shawn said.

"What are we looking for?"

"I don't know. That's what we have to find out."

The severely damaged Lincoln had been towed from the crash site by J.K. Towing and was temporarily laid to rest inside the well-lit, locked impound yard beside John Krueger's shop at the other end of town.

"I don't think we should try to get into that place," Steve said.

"Why?" Shawn asked, as if he suspected a streak of yellow had appeared down Steve's back.

"'Cause my dad does a lot of business with John, and I don't want to mess that up."

"Well, Watson, if you don't want to do it, I'll go alone."

"Now just hold on, Sherlock. Don't get your undies in a bundle. I think I know how to get some help with this one."

Shawn threw a puzzled stare. "What kind of help?"

"Lee. We'll get Lee to help us."

They knew Lee from High School, as a kid, carefree to the point of recklessness; he barely graduated a year earlier and was part of a different crowd. Other than an occasional "hello" in the Bowling Alley game room on Friday nights, Shawn rarely had any association with him. But Steve had; he had conned Lee into hauling the '56 Chevy into town for ten bucks, and since then, Lee frequently manned his father's tow truck, delivering disabled cars to Edgar's garage.

Shawn thought a long moment and then realized that Steve's idea seemed a bit safer than scaling an eight-foot high fence and risking the chance of getting caught.

9:30 p.m. was not too late to call the Krueger residence; it was the emergency after hours phone number for the towing service.

"Lee's not home... you might try the Bowling Alley."

"Thanks, John," Steve answered. "I'll find him there."

****

Sitting alone near the end of the long horseshoe bar, nursing a long-necked brown bottle, Lee Krueger looked more the part of a farm boy: tall, lean, broad-shouldered, handsome in a rugged sort of way, and as always, dressed in blue jeans and western shirt. He had all but extracted himself from most social circles, now that all of his High School buddies had moved away to jobs or the Military. His girlfriend had dumped him, and he had not fully recovered from the death of his only brother in Viet Nam.

Lee had slipped in and out of various moods lately, ranging from bad to worse; on some days, a junkyard dog might seem friendlier. He spent most of his days working at his father's shop – a combination towing service, used car lot, and as a sideline, John Krueger restored antique farm tractors, for which he was quite well-known. In his rather withdrawn state, Lee could only envy the lifestyles of others; he viewed himself as socially unacceptable, as he usually spent evenings alone, ignored by almost everyone.

From the side entrance, Steve spotted Lee at the bar. He approached cautiously, not knowing where Lee's current mood swing might have taken him. Shawn followed a few steps behind. To him, Lee represented a social speed bump.

"Hi, Lee," Steve offered, laying a friendly slap on Lee's back. He sat on the next barstool. "Your Dad said you might be here."

Shawn took a seat on the other side of Lee.

Lee produced a barely noticeable smile. "Allison, Kelly." He always addressed everyone by last name; it was his trademark.

Awed by their friendly advance, Lee reminded himself of his longtime admiration of the two guys sitting beside him – Shawn, for his intellect; Steve, for his physique. But he always kept those feelings to himself; he didn't think they would ever have any interest in his friendship, as they were both out of his league by social standards.

"Got that old Chevy runnin' yet?" Lee asked. It was the only link to anything he had in common with them.

"Naw," Steve answered. "Engine's shot. Dad is gonna try to find another one for us."

The comfort level gradually increased as they chatted about the old car. It wasn't long before Lee was curious to see the progress Shawn and Steve had made.

"'C'mon, let's go for a cruise," Steve suggested. "We can stop at Edgar's."

****

After a half-hour of randomly cruising around the back streets in Lee's Dodge pickup truck, the threesome had traversed more than just a few miles of blacktop; Shawn and Steve came to realize they had missed out on years with a good companion. Lee was no rocket scientist, but he possessed other genuine qualities that far outweighed his inabilities as a scholar. Lee was learning that there were exceptions to the social rules. New friendships spawned. It was just what they all needed.

****

"What's this?" Lee asked. He curiously eyed the five wedge-shaped, peculiar objects on the front seat of the old Chevy.

Shawn and Steve had forgotten they left the pieces there when they decided to look for Lee.

"Um, well, that's the reason we came looking for you," Shawn said. His confidence in Lee was building, and he decided it was safe, and perhaps necessary to let Lee in on their secrets. Lee wouldn't be a threat to their security, and he was their ticket into the impound yard.

"They're ancient artifacts," Steve added.

"If we tell you about them," Shawn said in a spy mystery whisper, "can you keep it a secret?"

"Sure," Lee responded. "Where'd they come from?"

"We don't know for sure, but you can help us find out."

"How?"

"Ya know that black Lincoln in your Dad's yard?"

"Yeah."

"Well, the guy that owns it is trying to steal these artifacts," Steve explained.

Shawn continued. "And there might be something in that Lincoln that will help us find out what they are."

Lee was already confused. Shawn realized a full explanation seemed necessary; he started at the beginning with Sara Fremont's accident, and then went on with the library break-in and the church escapade, and how the guy in the black Lincoln had chased them that night. He told Lee about the bizarre discovery they had made, and even though Lee didn't understand the whole concept, he seemed intrigued, and ecstatic, knowing he had just become the third Musketeer.

"So, what do you want me to do?" Excitement filled Lee's voice.

"We need you to get us into the yard so we can search the Lincoln."

Lee dug in his pockets. "I don't have my keys with me. How 'bout tomorrow night?"

"Tomorrow night will be just fine," Shawn beamed. "Let's make it about ten o'clock."

****

Living in a small town did have its advantages: by ten o'clock on a weeknight, the streets usually resembled a ghost town. Westland had gained a reputation over the years for its serenity; nothing evil ever occurred there, so Jake rarely patrolled much later than that.

Shawn and Steve were on patrol, though. The green Mustang sparkled passing under the lonely lights of a deserted Main Street as they kept a close eye on Krueger's place, watching for Lee's pickup. Jake's squad car sat in front of his house on Washington, nine blocks away. Other than a few house lights shining here and there, the town seemed to be asleep. The conditions appeared perfect.

When Lee's headlights turned into the driveway, Shawn and Steve were only a block away. Hearts raced. Adrenalin flowed. It wasn't just the possibility of a great discovery; it wasn't just answers that may lie hidden within the car. It was more than that. It was the mission itself. It was the excitement, the thrill.

A villain had evolved; he had proven his unfeigned desire to gain possession of the artifacts, and it seemed obvious, now, that he would not employ above-board diplomacy. By his devious acts, Taylor had confirmed that the artifacts were indeed valuable for some unknown reason, and he was willing to risk felonious behavior to get them.

Shawn and Steve had been threatened, violated, accosted. They could have easily sought the protection and assistance of the authorities, abruptly ending the madness. But this was *their* challenge. This was *their* battle. Unexplainable intrigue drove them beyond all limits to protect the cloak-and-dagger concept they didn't yet understand. It couldn't end – not just yet.

With a track record like theirs, the odds were stacked against them. The library break-in had resulted in a near bust; the church incident culminated in near disaster. Although they had emerged the victors, achieving the prescribed goals, and had escaped both times from sudden doom, a sinister, black, cataclysmatic cloud seemed to lurk in every shadow. One adversary was in jail, and the other in a hospital bed; certainly, neither of them could pose any threat now, but an element of stealth menace still breathed heavily in the dark.

"Better park your car 'round back," Lee suggested. "I'll unlock the gate and wait in front of the office." Lee was drawn into this spy vs. spy scheme now, too, even though he didn't have a clue about the objective.

Shawn stopped just short of where the security light reached, near the backside of the lot; Steve crouched beside him. They peered through the chain link fence at the smashed Lincoln, flanked on either side by equally useless, wrecked iron. A hazy yellow glow flooded the wrecks. It would be nearly impossible to remain concealed, once they were inside the fence.

"Maybe this is a waste of time," Shawn whispered.

Aborting this mission seemed as disgusting to Steve as kissing his sister. Turning back now would deprive them of yet another victory; quitting now rendered the impression of humiliating defeat. He couldn't accept that.

"But we're this close," Steve said.

Shawn didn't answer. He just stared at the wrecked car.

"We might not get another chance," Steve urged. "Won't know if we don't look."

He didn't wait for Shawn's approval. Steve trotted along the fence, looking up and down Main Street for passing cars. There were none. As he rounded the corner and headed toward the gate he noticed Lee standing next to his truck by the office door.

Lee caught a glimpse of Steve, and then Shawn following him. He made no gestures of pending danger. Steve pulled on the gate; opening it just enough to squeeze through, he sprinted into the Lincoln's shadow and crouched beside the passenger side door. When he turned to look back toward the gate, Shawn nearly fell on top of him, unable to stop the forward motion as quickly as Steve had.

They sat there in the shadow for a few moments listening and watching for movement. Someone would surely interrupt their investigation; who, how, and when they didn't know, but previous experience had taught them to be ready for anything.

"Okay, Sherlock," Steve whispered. "What are we looking for?"

Shawn shrugged his shoulders. "I don't know." He reached for the door handle, pushed the button in, and the door popped open slightly. No interior lights came on, which meant the battery was either dead or disconnected.

Steve poked his head up to the rear passenger door window. Seeing nothing but his reflection in the glass, he opened that door and crawled into the roomy back seat, pulling the door shut as quietly as possible. Shawn was already sprawled across the front seat, probing the floor with his penlight.

"See anything?" Steve asked.

"No, nothing but a gun under the seat." Shawn pulled himself up to see into the rear seat, shining the small light all around. There was nothing but a pair of muddy wingtip shoes sitting on a newspaper behind the drivers seat.

"Are the keys in the ignition?" Steve asked.

Shawn pointed the penlight at the dash; the keys were there.

"Let's look in the trunk," Steve said.

"Good idea, Watson." Shawn jerked the keys from the ignition switch and slid out onto the ground. Steve exited the rear door, and again they sat in the shadow, listening, waiting for any unknown surprises. When all seemed still, they cautiously crept to the rear of the car. Shawn held the flashlight while Steve worked the lock.

Two silhouettes leaned into the dark compartment; the force of the impact when the Lincoln slammed into the tree had dislodged and scattered the contents of a small suitcase, and partially hidden by the tangled mess of clothing, a brown leather briefcase. Shawn dug it out, snapped open the latch and began pawing through the many papers – maps and drawings, mostly. One sheet of onionskin caught his eye. The text typewritten, single-spaced, filled the page. Shawn zeroed the light in on the first few lines and began reading; Steve peeked around the open trunk lid, concentrating on the pair of headlights beaming across the lot in front of the gate.

"Shut off the flashlight and don't move," Steve whispered with insistence.

Deeply involved in the reading material, Shawn failed to comprehend the urgency right away.

"Turn off the light," Steve said again, this time nudging Shawn's arm. The trunk went black.

They could just barely hear Lee's voice, masked by an idling car motor.

"Can you see who it is?" Shawn whispered.

"Might be Jake. I think we'd better get outa here."

Shawn folded the paper, stuffed it in his hip pocket and looked over his shoulder toward the fence at the back of the lot.

"We can make it, easy," Steve whispered.

Not entirely in agreement with the idea, Shawn considered the difficulty in trying to explain why they were pillaging a Lincoln Town Car in the middle of the night. In comparison, the fence seemed less hazardous.

Steve lowered himself to hands and knees. "Follow me," he urged Shawn, and started for the back corner of the lot where they would be out of the line of sight from Lee and his visitor.

****

Lee raised his hand in a casual wave as the green Mustang cruised by on Main Street. Shawn couldn't tell if Jake had noticed them, but it didn't appear he had any intention of pursuit. Lee was keeping him occupied for the time being, and apparently he had drawn Jake's attention away from the open gate.

"Thanks, Lee," Shawn muttered, peering into the rear view mirror.

"That paper you found," Steve said. "What is it?"

"Looks like part of a letter… from some archeologist. In France, I think."

There hadn't been enough time at the wrecked car to read the entire page; Shawn reached for his hip pocket and pulled out the folded paper. He handed it to Steve, turned on the dome light and continued driving toward the lake.

"Here, read it," Shawn said. "I didn't get through it all."

On what appeared to be the second page of a letter, the writing clearly explained why the Professor was so interested in the artifacts, and why he had been possessed with evil obsession to gain their ownership.

Several years earlier, a team of archaeologists had been studying a dig site at the ruins of a Fourteenth Century cathedral, destroyed in a bombing raid during World War II, somewhere in northern France. There they uncovered a similar set of artifacts, but only four pieces. Their in-depth investigation, so far, had rendered no conclusions.

"And just listen to *this*," Steve said, quoting a passage from the letter. "We strongly believe *your* discovery of a fifth piece in America may be the missing link in our investigation."

"That bastard! He contacted them and never told Sara about it. And now he's taking the credit for the discovery."

"Kinda looks that way, don't it?"

Shawn nosed the Mustang up to a guardrail at the edge of the lake and stopped the motor. He grabbed the paper from Steve's lap, holding it so the dome light allowed him to see it better. Now he could read it without being disturbed.

For several silent minutes his eyes studied every line, calculated every word; rampant visions scurried about like rodents in a dark cellar. The facts still seemed vague; the letter defined only a sketchy outline that did little more than intensify the mystery. Unless they were withholding some information, the foreign scientists appeared to know even less; the physical description of their find was nearly identical to the pieces Shawn and Steve had recovered, but there was no mention of the reflecting properties, nor any peculiar energy detection.

"Whatever those things are," Shawn mumbled, staring through the windshield, "they're over six hundred years old."

"How do you know that?"

"These French guys found theirs in the ruins of a Fourteenth Century church. Do the math."

Steve pondered a long moment. "So why don't they know about the light reflecting thing?"

"Because they're scientists. They're probably studying those things in some fancy laboratory using all sorts of scientific equipment."

Steve squeezed out a puzzled grin.

"Think about it," Shawn explained. "We discovered that purely by accident. *They* don't have a shop light and a '56 Chevy."

Sara had never mentioned it, and Shawn couldn't recall anything in her forty-seven pages of research notes that she was aware of any other existing studies; the letter definitely confirmed Taylor's less-than-honorable intentions.

"We'd better destroy this letter," Shawn suggested. "I don't want to get caught with it."

Steve pulled a book of matches from his shirt pocket. They got out of the Mustang and sat on the guardrail. Steve struck the match; they watched the black ashes fall to the sand.

"Wanna go for a swim?"

****

Just a couple of days had passed when Woodrow Taylor arrived at J.K. Towing in a taxi, still feeling the effects from the accident. His left arm was in a sling, bright white tape across a broken nose, left eye blackened and swollen, and he walked with a pronounced limp. He was only there to collect his personal belongings left in the destroyed black car. He assured John Krueger that his insurance company would handle the towing and storage bill, and would dispose of the wreck.

As soon as the taxi whisked Taylor away, Lee reported the development to Shawn. Even though their main adversary would be occupied with recovery for a while, Shawn and Steve agreed that this wasn't the end of his ploy; security measures would have to remain strict. They had already proved their worthiness of meeting the Professor's challenges, so far, but they knew he'd probably launch another attack in time. The battle wasn't over. They loved it.

Since they had uncovered the letter from the French archeologists, they felt a new sense of challenge. The cloak-and-dagger game had progressed to a more prestigious level -- a team of highly trained and knowledgeable scientists versus a team of American youths, competing to find the origin and meaning of the unusual artifacts. The odds were in favor of the American youths. They had *all* the pieces, not damaged by World War II bombs, and they had advanced far beyond the discoveries of the Frenchmen with the aid of a simple shop light and a sheet of spray-painted cardboard. The only advantage the foreign scientists enjoyed was that they didn't have a crazed college professor breathing down their necks.

****

In just a few days, Lee had established a strong bond with his new friends, and began spending more time with them, even when they studied the artifacts. He didn't have a clue about what he was seeing as he viewed the mini light shows, but curiosity held his interest.

After several sessions of not noticing anything significant, Steve suggested they should find a new hiding spot for the wedges, just in case. Shawn agreed as he stuffed the pieces back into the bag. With the quickly approaching holiday weekend, there would be no time for any more experimentation for a while. Lee knew the perfect place at his house. No one would ever look for them there.

****

Thursday nights at the Public Library were usually quite busy, but this week there were only a half dozen patrons, at most, probably due to the upcoming holiday. Steve and Lee strolled in at seven o'clock -- they were anxious to start making plans for the weekend and the party at the lake.

July Fourth had become tradition for the current year graduates to throw one big bash at Jasper Lake; the event was intended as their final farewell to Westland High. Other non-seniors would be there, too -- girlfriends, boyfriends, and just friends – and that was okay. Shawn and Steve had earlier debated on attending, but then they realized this may be the last chance to see some of their classmates before they departed for college or jobs, just as Lee's friends had. Not only would they attend, they would *have fun*. Steve's eighteenth birthday was just a couple of days after the Fourth, so this would double as his unofficial birthday celebration as well. And somehow, it didn't seem right if Lee wasn't invited to join them.

With hardly any interruptions – except for old Mrs. Clark seeking a book on the care of her newly acquired parakeet -- the trio engineered the preparations for the big event. Shawn was pretty sure he would become the captive audience-of-one with his father's lecture on drinking and driving; Don knew what the graduation parties at the lake were all about. Shawn wanted to be one step ahead by volunteering to leave the Mustang at home... *before* his father engaged in the lecture.

It was almost eight o'clock and time to close when the phone rang.

"Public Library... this is Shawn."

The voice on the other end was distinctly familiar. "I trust you are still in possession of the five artifacts."

"Maybe."

"I am prepared to pay the sum of one thousand dollars... can we make a deal?"

Shawn didn't have to ponder long on the offer. "No... I don't think so." Taylor was the last person he would give them to, no matter how much he offered.

"In the name of science, it would be in your best interest--"

This time it was Shawn's turn to interrupt like a goose with a bad attitude. "In the name of science, you can kiss my ass."

"Very well... you will hear from me again very soon." Taylor hung up.

Steve was beginning to think that Shawn should have just accepted the offer. But Shawn was persistent, and quickly regained Steve's support. He wasn't ready to give in to this evil man who had created all the recent difficulties.

CHAPTER 12

The Fourth was ushered in under a dismal, gray sky, and although the early morning shower that barely settled the dust was a welcomed gift from above, everyone hoped the sunny, pleasant forecast would prevail. By mid-morning, gloom gave way to the day that had been promised; the meteorologists were spared from embarrassment. The rain was just enough to give the flowerbeds a perky glow, and the air was fresh and clean.

Another customary annual event on that day was a back yard barbecue at the Kellys' -- invitations had been extended to all the lumberyard employees, other businessmen around town, friends and neighbors. It wasn't unusual to see thirty or forty people show up, and it always proved to be a joyous gathering. Don Kelly was feeling a bit uneasy about how he would respond to queries from the arriving guests, regarding the situation in which his brother, Andy, was involved. A larger-than-expected turnout was gathering; so far, no one was speaking of the incident, and as the afternoon evolved into a typical July Fourth festivity, Don sensed the support of his friends and neighbors.

Shawn spent the better part of the afternoon entertaining the younger children with badminton and whiffle ball. But when Richard and Steve Allison appeared, Shawn and Steve soon became the stars of the volleyball court, as the other adults were no match for their agility. When it came to pitching horseshoes, though, the more experienced old pros proved they were still capable of being the dominant figures.

Lee Krueger's pickup was parked in the driveway when Steve and Shawn returned from the house after a quick shower and donning clean clothes. Lee was enjoying a juicy burger from the grill. Shawn approached his father and quietly announced that he and Steve were about to leave for the lake. Just as he anticipated, the dreaded lecture began; he rolled his eyes as required by the laws of teenage behavior. "Yes Dad," and to avoid further verbal punishment, he volunteered all the information: "The Mustang is staying in the garage. We're riding with Lee and we're camping overnight at the beach."

That satisfied Don's concerns. "Well, then, have a good time."

****

The lake beach was already crowded, and parking space was at a premium. To date, this was the largest class graduating from Westland High, and no doubt, this was the biggest gathering Jasper Valley had ever accommodated. The atmosphere left little room to deny that this mass of seniors was about to give themselves a spectacular send-off. The beach party was the main event, the centerpiece of the day's celebration, the very pinnacle of that once-in-a-lifetime milestone – High School graduation; it was their self-administered merit, earned with the last four years of their lives.

The huge bonfire blazing on the beach was being fed from a heaping pickup truckload of split wood backed up to the edge of the sand. Another car was along side the truck, doors open, and a powerful stereo was pouring out the local radio station's signal. *The Beatles* had been at the top of the charts for some time, and this station -- like every other pop format station in the country -- was taking full advantage of the Brits' popularity. It was a sure bet, though, that later on, after the sun went down, Chicago's *WLS* would become the station of choice; the controversial but popular deejay, Dick Biante, would rock n' roll the crowd well into the wee hours.

So far, aside from the near constant volley of Blackcats, Cherry Bombs, M-80's, and the occasional whistle of a bottle rocket echoing through the valley, the group was well behaved. To those kids, drugs were a commodity obtained from the pharmacy when someone was sick, and marijuana or LSD weren't even in their vocabulary. But B-E-E-R was, and there was no shortage of that. And for certain, they could expect a surprise visit by at least one County Deputy sometime during the night. Jasper Lake beach, however, provided plenty of dark hiding places for those who were not yet that magical age of eighteen.

This was the second party of its kind that Lee had attended, and naturally he felt a little out of place at this one, even though almost everyone greeted him and made every attempt to make him feel welcome. Shawn and Steve assured him they were glad he had joined them for their special occasion.

By the time they each popped open their third can of Budweiser, the multitude once concentrated around the fire had dispersed into various groups: the jocks and cheerleaders, the home-ec sissies, the red-necks, the scholars, and then there were the pyrotechnics who kept everybody aware it was still

Independence Day. Shawn or Steve weren't too eager to join the ranks of any of them, so they and Lee lugged their cooler full of refreshments to a less crowded spot away from the noisy assemblage.

Shawn was beginning to show the initial signs of a Bud buzz when he announced that Mother Nature was calling. "I hafta lake a teak... I mean... take a leak." The other two giggled at the jumbled statement and just watched as he carefully threaded his way through the maze of coolers, blankets, and lawn chairs, and then disappeared into the darkness beyond the fire.

A half hour had passed when Steve and Lee decided to look for him, but Shawn was making himself scarce, and they didn't know why. It wasn't Shawn's nature to abandon anyone, and especially Steve. They checked the truck... no Shawn. They mingled with the classmates for a while, and then finally returned to the cooler. Steve was mildly frustrated. "He's got to be here somewhere... we just missed him somehow."

Lee offered some speculation. "Maybe he hooked up with some chick and they took off."

Steve scanned the crowd. "I doubt that... very much." He kept scanning, then concluded, "Shawn's a big boy... he'll come back when he's ready."

By three a.m. they had consumed the contents of the cooler. The crowd had diminished to a third of its original number. Die-hards remained circled around the fire; many were snuggled into sleeping bags. The fireworks were all spent, the stereo was quiet, and the smoke from the slowly dying blaze drifted across the moonlit lake surface. The graduating class of 1966 had bid its glorious, final farewell.

Steve and Lee retrieved three sleeping bags from the truck, optimistically anticipating the return of their lost companion, stretched out on the beach and fell asleep. What had started out as a special night had ended in disappointment -- at least for Steve.

****

What seemed to be an eternity, Shawn laid curled up in the trunk of a new-smelling car for over an hour, in absolute darkness, so trying to see the face of his wristwatch was useless. His first thoughts had been that he was the unsuspecting victim of some sort of joke after being grabbed from behind and stuffed into the trunk by two guys much bigger and stronger than him. The car had slowed and stopped only momentarily a few times. Each time it did, he thought it would be the grand finale, and he would soon learn the point of the prank, and his fate. But now the car had been traveling at highway speed for a long time, and he was beginning to panic emotionally; his struggle to break free had been answered much to aggressively to be just a prank, and his cries of resistance had apparently gone unnoticed amidst the party noise.

His imagination ran rampant, envisioning how his body would be found floating in a swamp somewhere. He thought about his family -- his Mustang –

Steve -- the library – college – family -- Steve. It was a kaleidoscope of his whole life, tumbling over and over, again and again. Occasionally, he could hear voices from inside the car and static from the radio as it was tuned from station to station. Psychologically exhausted, he drifted into an unsettled sleep.

The abrupt sound of a car door slamming shut brought him only to semi-consciousness. As he listened to the noise of an electric garage door closing, his only thought was, "what a weird dream." The door closer stopped and all was silent for a few seconds. Then another car door slammed, and there was the brief zipping sound of a key being inserted into the trunk lock. Before his eyes could adjust to the light, two strong hands grabbed his forearms and two more on his ankles. They hoisted him up out of the trunk and stood him beside the car without releasing the grip on his arms. "What the hell is goin' on?" An angry fear was in his voice; he still couldn't get a good look at the two brutes manhandling him, but he was quite sure they were total strangers – nothing about either of them seemed recognizable. Shawn attempted to struggle free, but his captors seemed twice his size and there were two of them. He quickly realized there was little chance of escape.

"We ain't gonna hurt ya," one of them said. "But you gotta shut up and do what we say... okay?" The other man began feeling Shawn's pants pockets. Shawn felt his wallet slip out. "If it's money you're after you ain't gonna find much there."

"We ain't after money... Shawn D. Kelly," the man said as he eyed the driver's license in the opened wallet. He then dug into Shawn's front pockets, pulled them inside out, and spilled their contents onto the floor at Shawn's feet. After determining nothing of importance was there, he said to his partner, "We'd better blindfold him before we take him to the house."

"Good idea... get something." The first man wasn't about to let go of the grip on Shawn's arms.

A bone-chilling click echoed through the nearly empty garage as Shawn caught a glimpse of the shiny switchblade coming toward him. He thought the worst and held his breath. One hand pulled the bottom of Shawn's muscle shirt away from his belly as the razor-sharp steel sliced through the fabric from the waist up to the neckline, then one by one, cut the straps over each shoulder. Another sharp chill raced through his bared torso as he watched the stranger twirl the shirt into a rope and tie it around Shawn's head, covering his eyes into total darkness once more.

"Okay. How's that?" one of the strangers said. "Let's go."

They guided Shawn through a doorway. They were outside, perhaps on a sidewalk. Shawn had no idea where he was, or where he was headed, but he was quite certain this wasn't Disneyland, and these guys weren't Mickey's welcoming committee. He could hear the distant hum of traffic, and the roar of a jet overhead. A door opened in front of him; they were soon inside again, negotiating down a flight of steps. The interior of the house smelled musty;

Shawn could tell it was a rather large house by the distance they had walked, but none of his senses detected anything familiar about it.

The painfully tight grip on his arms guided him through another doorway, and then commanded him to stop. Soft, soothing classical violins sharply contrasted the frightening situation.

"Here's your boy."

As he heard those words, Shawn's imagination went wild again; the image of all sorts of horrible acts flashed before him. Was he ever going to be seen again by his family and friends? Just then a hand pulled away the blindfold.

"Ahh... we meet again young Mr. Kelly."

Shawn squinted and blinked, trying to adjust to the light. The fuzziness began to solidify; the room manifested and the human shape standing before him slowly came into focus. Like the final letters of a crossword puzzle discovered, the mystery of the past few hours was now crystal clear as he stared at the obnoxious, half-baked smirk on the gray-haired man's face.

"I'm sure, by the looks of things, Tommy and Curtis have caused your journey to be a bit unpleasant. Is there anything I can get for you?"

Shawn was temporarily overtaken by the polite kindness being offered. "I... I'd like a glass of water, please... and I sure could use a cigarette."

More hospitality poured out -- this time, somewhat commanding. "One of you fetch Mr. Kelly some water and a pack of cigarettes... and for God's sake get the poor lad a shirt."

CHAPTER 13

The hot morning sun beating down on the beach awakened Steve and Lee at nine o'clock. A few of the leftover partiers who had braved the night elements began to stir as well. Only one of them had any recollection of seeing Shawn -- he had also been in the shadows relieving his bladder. As they were walking back to the bonfire, he had heard someone call out Shawn's name, and Shawn had turned and headed for the parking lot. "That was the last I saw of him... I just thought it was one of you."

Steve speculated that even though it seemed odd, maybe Shawn *had* left with someone else, and he was probably already at home.

****

Kathy Kelly was retrieving a stack of envelopes from the mailbox at the end of the driveway as Lee's Dodge truck pulled in. She was a little surprised that her son was not accompanying his friends. Lee stood quietly as Steve spoke to Mrs. Kelly. "Shawn left the lake last night with someone else. He's probably up in his room sleeping." Kathy invited the boys into the kitchen where she offered each a cold can of soda from the refrigerator. Lee sat at the table while Steve bolted up the stairs to Shawn's bedroom where he was confident he would find Shawn. The bed had not been disturbed. Confused, he returned to the kitchen. Kathy was staring at a sheet of paper with a puzzled look. Her voice became nearly hysterical. "What the... MY GOD! SHAWN... THEY'VE KIDNAPPED SHAWN!"

Kathy's excitement startled Steve. "What? Who?" He examined the paper. The short typewritten message centered on the page was simple:

> *"WE HAVE YOUR SON. HE HAS NOT BEEN HARMED. HE IS IN NO DANGER AT THIS TIME. DO NOT CONTACT POLICE. YOU WILL RECEIVE FURTHER INSTRUCTIONS SOON."*

Frantic, Kathy could hardly get the words out when she phoned Don at the lumberyard. Don didn't know the reason, but by the tone of her voice he did know there must be some urgency in her request for him to come home immediately.

Don entered the kitchen to find his wife sitting at the table crying, and Steve attempting to comfort her. Don embraced her. "What's wrong? Where's Shawn?" He glared at Steve.

Kathy was unable to speak; Steve held up the note, offering it to Don. In disbelief, Don laughed. "This must be some sort of joke... this doesn't happen in Westland." He turned to the two boys with a stare, as if he suspected them of some mischief. Steve explained how Shawn had just disappeared from the lake party, and when he hadn't returned by morning, they thought he must have come home during the night. He seemed too serious for Don to continue thinking he was making up any part of the story.

The Kellys were not suffering financially, to say the least, but they weren't so wealthy that anyone would view them as a worthwhile target of extortion. Who could possibly be responsible for such an act?

Reality set in. Don announced his intentions to call Jake, but Steve stepped in with a desperate reminder -- he too, was fearful for his best friend's safety. "No! The note says not to call the police... if you do, maybe they'll... maybe they'll hurt Shawn."

A picture of the conversation he and Shawn had had one night, with Steve as the main subject, flashed back in Don's mind. There would be no better time to set aside his uneasy feelings toward his son's friend. "You might be right... but we have to do *something.*"

Steve was an expert at quick thinking, and he already had a plan in mind. Not knowing if they really were being watched, Lee would have the best opportunity to get to Jake without being detected.

Lee absorbed his instructions and in no time was at his father's shop calling the County Sheriff's Office, requesting Jake to be dispatched right away to J.K. Towing.

It seemed to be a rather unusual assignment, but Jake had known Don Kelly nearly his whole life and he trusted that Don wouldn't lure him into a dangerous position without having a good reason. Although Jake insisted on an explanation, Lee stuck to his sworn commitment. "Go to the Kellys' house, *out of uniform* and in your own *personal car* -- *not* the squad car. Don't radio to headquarters where you are going... can't tell you why, but it's *really* important. You'll find out when you get there."

Not knowing what to expect, Jake was reluctant, but he respected the wishes of the prominent citizen and responded just as he had been instructed. His first reaction, too, was one of disbelief and overwhelming amazement with an occurrence that didn't seem possible in *this* town. But Shawn *was* missing; his friends didn't know where or how; a threatening note found in the mailbox confirmed the validity of the situation.

Jake had never dealt with a kidnapping, but common sense told him to explore all the possibilities first. He instructed Steve to start calling every one of their classmates who might know of Shawn's whereabouts without revealing why he was asking. There was an outside chance this was a prank, and Jake wanted to cover that base before it got out of hand. Steve grabbed the phone book and began making the calls.

Don, Kathy, and Jake sat down at the kitchen table and tried to piece together what little information they had. Shawn had made no mention of any problems recently; he was a pretty well adjusted kid so there wasn't much reason to believe he would have manufactured this scenario to disguise a runaway. And none of the family had any enemies – period. Pending any information Steve might gather on the phone, Jake decided the best place to start an investigation was at the lake where Shawn was last seen. He knew how to attain the necessary help and still remain discreet. Steve could keep making the calls, and Lee Krueger could show him what he needed to know at the lake.

****

Shawn sat directly across a four-foot square table from the man responsible for his abduction. A paper tub full of deep-fried chicken, another smaller container of mashed potatoes and gravy, a plastic fork wrapped in cellophane, and two pint cartons of milk sat on the table in front of him.

"I had my assistant get you some chicken from the Colonel... I hope you like chicken."

Shawn just stared at the food; he wanted to resist, but his stomach growled. Taylor pushed the containers closer to Shawn. "Go ahead. Eat… there's plenty... you must be hungry by now." Taylor's voice was cheerful.

Shawn couldn't resist any longer, and hesitantly plucked a chicken leg from the tub and took a bite. He was curiously suspicious of Taylor's pleasing attitude, certainly the opposite of that which he had observed during the previous encounter that night at the church. He wasn't going to volunteer any conversation, but he *would* satisfy the hunger with the banquet his *host* was providing.

"Good! We'll talk when you have finished dining." Taylor left the room.

Shawn had fallen asleep about the break of dawn on a cot, locked in the ten-by-ten basement room. There were no windows. The walls were bare wood paneling, and besides the cot, the only furnishings were the small table, two wooden chairs, and a lamp. He looked at his watch; it was 3:30. He had been sleeping most of the day. And now that he had some food in his stomach, he thought he felt pretty good, considering. He pushed his chair back away from the table, took a cigarette from the pack and lit it, as Taylor entered the room and sat down where he had been before.

"Did you enjoy your meal? I hope it was to your liking."

Shawn stared at Taylor's chest, trying not to make direct eye contact for a few seconds. "It was okay."

"Good." A wide grin occupied Taylor's face. "Now, we have some unfinished business to discuss. Are you ready to do that now?"

Shawn looked up into Taylor's eyes. "Maybe." Somehow, he knew it wasn't going to do much good to ask any questions at this point, so he would just listen for now.

"Very well... first of all, I want to tell you that surely by now your family has found the note my assistants left in your mailbox. That note stated your well-being. I hope they aren't too alarmed. I instructed them *not* to alert the authorities. I trust they love their son enough to heed those instructions."

A chill went down Shawn's spine; the feeling of safety he had managed to build over the past hour was rapidly diminishing, and a distinct look of fear appeared in his eyes.

Taylor continued. "Don't worry, Shawn. I really don't want to harm you."

Shawn couldn't hold back. "Then why did you have those goons haul me here in the trunk of a car like a dog? And where am I anyway?"

Taylor went on calmly. "I am truly sorry for any discomforts you encountered. And it is not important for you to know where you are. Unfortunately, it will be necessary to transport you back home in the same manner to avoid you knowing where you have been, however, we will do our best at making that ride a little more comfortable. In the meantime, I will make every effort to make your stay here a pleasant one."

Shawn gritted his teeth. "So what is it you want from me?" He already knew the answer to that question, but maybe it would get Taylor to the point a little quicker.

"What I want is the set of artifacts you have obtained, and so cleverly deprived me of."

"I'm *not* giving you the artifacts. Sara..."

"Sara Fremont..." Taylor interrupted as he often did, "... promised to accompany me, with the piece she had at the time, to a meeting with other scientists to perform a study critical to... well, that's not important. But now, Ms. Fremont has passed on. The artifacts are rightfully mine."

"Well you ain't gettin' them."

"I anticipated your unwillingness to cooperate. A second set of instructions has already been sent to your home regarding their delivery to me. As soon as I have them in my possession, you will be returned to your home. And by the time you arrive there, I will be in... well, it's not important for you to know that, either. I'm afraid the decision to let me get the artifacts is out of your hands."

"You'll be in France. And what makes you think I won't blow the whistle on you?"

Taylor was taken by complete surprise that this kid seemed to know a fact he had been so carefully protecting. "I think we've discussed enough for one day. We'll continue this conversation at a later time." He abruptly stood and walked out the door, locking it behind him.

Shawn plucked another piece of chicken from the tub, stretched out on the cot, and chuckled under his breath. He knew he had struck a vulnerable spot. Maybe the ball was back in his court.

****

Within an hour, Jake's contacts arrived at the lake beach. FBI Agents Bill Sorenson and Terry Peters were of a special division of the bureau that primarily engaged in abduction investigations. They agreed with Jake's decision to initiate this investigation with a search of the abduction site. The beach and adjacent area, now void of any activity, produced nothing, however. Too many cars and people had tracked over anything that might have been there. Only typical party debris was left behind. Lee assured the officers that no one had been swimming the night before, so the possibility of a drowning was quickly ruled out.

By sundown, a large enough area surrounding the beach had been combed inch by inch to satisfy the investigators that there was nothing to be found. Jake and Lee returned to the Kelly home. The two strangers driving a pickup truck followed them in, taking Don by surprise. They were dressed casually, appearing more like building contractors than FBI agents. Jake introduced the men. Upon learning their status, Don expressed his concern of the warning they received regarding authority contact.

"Don't worry" Sorenson said. "This is our job. We deal with cases like this all the time... we know how to handle this kind of situation."

In a take-charge tone, Sorenson demanded everyone to take a seat around the kitchen table as Agent Peters opened a brief case, out of which he removed a small battery operated tape recorder and a notebook. Steve and Lee quickly took their places beside Jake, Don, and Kathy. Peters spoke clearly into the recorder: "July fifth, nine thirty-seven p.m., the Don Kelly residence, rural

Westland," and then instructed each person at the table to speak their full names into the microphone.

For the next hour, every detail was discussed, with particular attention given to Steve's description of the previous night's chain of events. Sorenson occasionally studied the abductor's note.

When the agents determined they had gathered ample information regarding the actual event, they suggested that the non-residents of the household should go home. There was nothing more Steve, Lee, or Jake could provide, and now time was needed to conduct a more confidential interview with the Kellys. The instructions to those leaving were quite explicit: "Don't discuss this matter with *anyone* -- not even your families." The last thing they wanted happening now was for the story to leak out and finding themselves surrounded by an army of bloodthirsty media reporters.

Steve wasn't satisfied with being shuffled out the door. His best friend had been kidnapped; he felt the need to be near. "If it's okay with you, I'd like to stay here... is that okay, Mr. Kelly? I can call my Dad and let him know I'm here."

Don looked at the agents with questioning eyes. "You know? I think I'd like that, too. He can sleep in Shawn's room."

Sorenson nodded his approval of the request.

After Jake and Lee left, Sorenson directed Steve to turn in for the night. The agents needed to gather a lot of personal information from the Kellys, and Don and Kathy might feel less hesitant to supply the answers without an outsider present. Disappointed that he would not be included in further discussion, Steve realized this was an important part of ensuring Shawn's safety; reluctantly, he trudged off to the upstairs bedroom.

From Shawn's room, he could hear the conversation continuing in the kitchen. He couldn't make out every word -- only bits and pieces: "...Text book abduction... not much to go on yet... wait for another contact... ransom arrangement..."

He rubbed his hand back and forth across the patchwork quilt. The sweet fragrance of the cologne that Shawn always wore still remained on the pillowcase. He had been gone less than twenty-four hours, but Steve already missed his best friend. What would it be like when Shawn left for college? Worse yet, what if he never returned now? Emotionally crushed by the fear dominating his thoughts, Steve settled back on the pillow and stared at the ceiling.

It was going to be a long, agonizing night for the Kellys; their only son had been kidnapped, and nobody knew why. Never before had they felt so helpless, or so violated. Urging them to try to get some rest, Sorenson assured them that their feelings were quite rational, and that by the next morning, he and his partner would have everything well organized and would be ready to combat whatever developed.

****

The sound of voices coming from downstairs woke Steve at 7:30 a.m. With all the excitement of the distressing current events, the thought never occurred to him that this was July sixth -- his birthday. It was day two of the nightmare he wanted to end, and his thoughts of Shawn's fate took precedence over all else. As he entered the kitchen, still groggy from a restless night, the FBI men, Don and Kathy were already gathered around the table drinking coffee. Mrs. Kelly offered to make him anything he wanted for breakfast, but he was content with only a large glass of orange juice.

Sorenson advised Don to go to the lumberyard and discreetly inform all his employees of the situation, and that they were not to phone the Kelly residence. He could then return home; he should be there for any further developments.

"I should probably go talk to my Dad, too," Steve said meekly.

Sorenson realized the close bond between Steve and Shawn. There was no reason to prevent contact with his father, but he did emphasize the importance of restricting comments to anyone else. Steve assured him that he wasn't about to do or say anything that would jeopardize Shawn's safety.

By mid-morning, Sorenson and Peters had everything coordinated. There was now additional undetectable surveillance of the Kelly home and the lumberyard. Even though they had no idea where Shawn was being held, they had the ability to facilitate immediate dispatch of colleagues to any location in the country. And if a time element became critical, they had at their disposal large sums of cash in the event that Don would incur any difficulty in assembling an enormous ransom. A wiretap was placed on the phone, both at the Kelly home and the lumberyard, to monitor incoming calls. Another FBI Agent posing as a bookkeeping auditor was in place at Kelly Lumber, and in case of social calls, Kathy had a prepared list of excuses for why she couldn't stay on the phone. Shawn very rarely received phone calls, but there was an excuse for his absence, as well. Everything was in place; now it was just a matter of waiting for the next contact from the kidnappers.

Don sorted through the daily stack of mail -- nothing but bills, junk mail, ad pamphlets, and several Thank You notes from friends who had attended the recent barbecue.

The rest of the day, Don and Kathy spent most of the time consoling one another. Occasionally, Kathy puttered around the kitchen, making sandwiches and coffee for her guests. Don attempted to tackle some business paperwork, but found it difficult to concentrate. It was impossible for either of them to direct their thoughts to anything other than what was happening to them right then.

Sorenson and Peters continued to study their notes, and listened to the recorded interviews from the previous night. They looked at maps, and went over plans for speculated scenarios. A lot of possibilities existed, and they wanted to be ready for anything.

Several times during the afternoon, the phone rang. Each time, the two Agents jumped into position with their listening and recording apparatus, and each time at least two hearts in the Kelly household nearly stopped as Kathy picked up the receiver. But every call resulted in the delivery of one of the prepared excuses.

As the evening hours set in, Richard and Steve pulled into the driveway. Don eagerly welcomed them inside, as Richard extended his sympathy, and added assurance to Sorenson that he or Steve had not breathed a word to anyone. Steve continued by explaining their presence. "Dad just took me out for my birthday dinner, and I knew you didn't want anyone calling here, so we wanted to stop by to see if anything... if Shawn is..." He was having trouble getting it out.

Don put a friendly arm around Steve's shoulders. "No, we haven't heard anything yet." He tried lifting the boy's broken spirit. "And Happy Birthday! Shawn mentioned it a couple days ago, but I guess I forgot... sorry we don't have a present."

Steve looked directly into Don's eyes. "The only present I want is for Shawn to come home safely." A tear trickled down one cheek; he wiped it away with the back of his hand.

Mr. Kelly pulled him closer with a one-arm hug. "You can stay again tonight if you want." He looked at Richard, winked, and continued. "Kathy can bake you a cake. She needs something to do."

Richard nodded his approval.

Kathy poured everyone coffee and they adjourned to the living room. They didn't want to disturb the array of papers, maps and books covering the kitchen table. A short time after they had gotten comfortable, Sorenson joined the group. He and his partner had made some speculative conclusions after reviewing several similar past cases. The wording of the note left in the mailbox indicated to them that Shawn wasn't in any immediate danger -- the kidnapper would have referred to something more specific if he intended to harm his hostage, and if this were a violent act, he wouldn't have bothered to leave a note at all. The note was left so that it would be found only after the perpetrators had plenty of time to reach a hideaway, perhaps a long distance from there. The mailbox was the perfect spot; it was certain the note would be found, but not until the next day. And it was not uncommon for two, three, maybe four days to pass, waiting to receive more contact. That was a typical kidnapper's method of creating high levels of anxiety in the victim's family to make them more willing to comply with demands.

Sorenson didn't tell them anything they hadn't already figured out. But hearing him say Shawn wasn't in any danger eased the tension just a little. It didn't change the fact, though, that they were all quite worried.

****

Shawn accepted the fact he wasn't going to escape the bonds of the guarded dungeon. He hadn't been outside the room since he was imprisoned, except for five or ten minutes at a time, periodically, to use an adjacent bathroom, during which time he was closely guarded by Tommy or Curtis. Over the past couple of days, he made several requests for items to help pass the time; each time there was a changing of the guard, they brought him magazines, candy bars, and Pepsi, but his petition for a radio was denied. Taylor knew the lad was smart enough to determine the geographic location by hearing radio broadcasts, so instead, a portable phonograph and a stack of LPs from Tommy's own private collection provided the next best alternative to satisfy Shawn's desire for music.

Shawn remained puzzled over the hospitality. He still believed Taylor must be an evil creature, but he was also convinced that nothing bad would happen if Taylor got what he wanted. Perhaps it *was* best to just cooperate, as he was beginning to feel impatient with confinement, and the sooner he was freed from this place, the better.

Visions of the artifacts disturbed him now. He thought of all the trouble he had gone through obtaining them, and the potential dangers and risks he and Steve had faced to protect their safekeeping. He thought of how close they had come to making a breakthrough discovery that could mean a passport to recognition, and a future that didn't include two-by-fours. But all that seemed useless now that Taylor controlled the outcome.

At suppertime, Taylor carried in a white paper bag bearing the familiar golden arches logo containing a large cup of soda, a *Big Mac*, and French fries. Shawn didn't hesitate this time to accept the fare. Taylor again sat down opposite Shawn. "We'll get right to the point," he said as he watched the teen munch on the fries. Shawn just listened.

"I don't know *where* you got the ridiculous notion I would be going to France." Taylor paused, hoping this bluff would draw out any further information; he wanted to find out just how much Shawn really knew. But Shawn recognized the scheme, and he wasn't about to reveal that he had read the letter in Taylor's brief case. He remained silent.

"Well, obviously you were just guessing." Taylor paused again, and still no verbal response from Shawn was aroused. He went on. "My wife left me years ago, and I have been living alone in this big house ever since. I have recently decided to sell the mansion, pack up my belongings and relocate to another part of the world... ah... perhaps South America. All the necessary arrangements have been made, and as soon as I have acquired the artifacts, I will commence my long awaited travel. By tomorrow night, I will be on a plane, *with the artifacts* in my brief case. Several hours later, my trusted assistants will escort you back to a location near your home, and you will never see them again. Trust me, Mr. Kelly, there is *nothing* you can do *this time* to stop me."

As he left the room, Taylor stopped and turned back toward Shawn.

"Oh, by the way. I have some friends at the University of Wisconsin who can make your time there either quite successful, *or quite unpleasant*. The choice is up to you."

CHAPTER 14

Friday, July 7th was like any other summer day, except that day the streets of Westland were beginning to buzz with rumors in wholesale proportions, as the local citizenry had many eyebrows raised. As in any small town, it would be unusual for irregular activity to go unnoticed. Don Kelly had not shown up at the cafe for his early morning coffee breaks, nor had he been at the lumberyard for two days, and his employees acted strangely when asked why. Kathy Kelly was being very short with anyone who phoned her. The library had not been open and no one had seen Shawn. His car wasn't in the driveway; it was behind a closed garage door, and instead, an unfamiliar pickup parked in its place. And then, Steve Allison was seen at the grocery store driving Don Kelly's pickup, and buying twice the groceries he usually did. Surely something was amiss, and not even Jake was saying anything.

Sorenson sent Steve to the store with a fifty-dollar bill and a shopping list. Kathy's unstable state of emotion wasn't conducive to the necessary security, so it wasn't a good idea for her to do the shopping, and although she insisted to pay for the food, Sorenson refused; he had an unlimited expense account, and he and his associate were appreciative of the delicious meals they ordinarily missed on assignments like this.

****

There was no return address on the plain, heavy brown envelope among the usual stack of mail -- only the Kellys' typewritten address, a stamp, and a Rochester, Minnesota postmark. Sorenson examined the outside of the envelope and concluded that the address may have been applied with the same typewriter used on the first note. With a razor knife, he carefully separated the sealed flap, not to disturb the contents. He wanted to preserve any evidence inside, *if* this was actually the contact they were awaiting. As he removed the paper, a key dropped from between the folds and onto the table. "Don't anyone touch that," he commanded as he unfolded the letter.

Unemotional, his keen eyes scanned the paper; his silence, a catalyst for the others' tension. "This is it," he said softly.

Peters stepped quickly to Sorenson's side; they studied the page without saying a word.

"Well what does it say?" Don asked anxiously.

Both Agents displayed puzzled faces. "These are very explicit instructions," Sorenson said. "But the abductor is *not* demanding money."

Peters carefully moved the key to the end of the table beside his brief case, examined it with a magnifying lens, and then began dusting it for fingerprints. Sorenson continued scrutinizing every word of the message. Don picked up the envelope, and looked once more at the postmark. "Well, at least we know what city Shawn is in."

Sorenson kept studying the paper and spoke at the same time. "My experience tells me that's a diversion. Anytime a kidnapper uses the mail as his method of contact, he almost always deposits it into the system where it will receive a postmark other than where he actually is, so as to get the police running off looking in the wrong direction, thus, easing the pressure on his real location."

Agent Peters broke in. "There's nothing on this key."

Sorenson proceeded with his analysis as though he were reading it from a book. "It's my assumption that your son is in the Twin Cities, probably somewhere within easy access to the airport. It seems to be the pattern. He was abducted from a beach party right under the noses of a hundred people, and the abductor is demanding the ransom be delivered to a locker at a busy airport at a busy time. It's obvious he is using mass confusion as his cover. Shawn is more than likely being held in a high population area where the police aren't apt to notice slightly out-of-the-ordinary activity... and I do know that he's okay... the abductor practically spells out when and how he will be released."

Don and Kathy were amazed that Sorenson could draw all those conclusions so quickly. "You said they don't want money... what *do* they want?" Don asked.

Peters responded to the inquiry. "Usually, ransoms are cash -- *large* sums of cash. Or sometimes child custody in the case of a divorce battle, and we've even dealt with abductors demanding the release of political prisoners. But you're going to have to help us out with this one. He's asking for five artifact pieces. Do you know what he means?"

The Kellys were dumbfounded. They stared at one another for a long moment with wrinkled brows. "No, I don't know," said Don.

Kathy added, "We don't have *any* antiques in our house... at all. Nothing of any *value.*"

Don stared at the paper where Sorenson was pointing out the lines in question. "I have no idea what that means."

Sorenson looked at his watch. "Well, we better figure it out. We've only got ten hours to deliver whatever it is to the Minneapolis Airport."

They sat around the kitchen table as Steve came in carrying two large bags of groceries. He thought it a little odd that he was being totally ignored when he struggled with the parcels as he placed them on the countertop. Peters was trying to jog the Kellys' memories. "Could it be jewelry? Or maybe some old pottery? They're small items. He says to package them in a box eight inches square."

Steve listened to the conversation, then interrupted. "Is this about Shawn? Have you heard something?"

"Yes," Don answered. "The kidnapper is demanding five artifacts as ransom, and we don't know what he means."

Steve's face paled. He had all but forgotten about the five wedges, and not once during this whole ordeal had he made the connection. "I know what they are."

It took a few seconds for Steve's statement to sink in, and then, like a swarm of honeybees attracted to a flowering rose bush, Sorenson, Peters, Don and Kathy surrounded him with questioning, intimidating stares.

"Why didn't you say something earlier?" Don drilled.

"I'm sorry," Steve pleaded with them. His eyes darted from one face to another in search of redemption. "I didn't think of it until just now when you mentioned the artifacts."

"Okay," Sorenson intervened. "Let's all calm down, and Steve, tell me what you know. We don't have a lot of time."

Steve described the pieces to the best of his recollection, and drew a crude diagram on a sheet of paper, explaining how Shawn had been secretly studying them.

"Where did they come from?" Sorenson asked.

To avoid getting himself or Shawn in trouble over their recent escapades, Steve simply replied, "From Sara."

"Who's Sara?"

"Sara was the librarian. She was killed about a month ago in a hit and run." Glancing at Mr. Kelly, Steve didn't want to cause any undue embarrassment by dwelling on that subject. "The person responsible for that is in jail."

"Where did Sara get them?"

"The church attic… a long time ago."

"Where are they now?"

"We hid them at Lee's place."

"Why?"

"'Cause there's some guy trying to get them away from Shawn."

"Who?"

"Can't remember his name. Shawn said it once, but I can't remember it now."

"How do you know he's trying to get them?"

"He's been calling Shawn at the library, and one night he chased us and..." Steve suddenly realized he had just gotten himself deeper into the facts than he wanted to be.

"And what?"

"...We got away from him. That's when we decided to hide them."

"Have you seen this man since? How about at the lake party?"

"No. Haven't seen him since then."

"Can you describe the man?"

"I only saw him once -- at night -- it was dark. I didn't get a good look at him."

"Can you get the artifacts and bring them here?"

"I can call Lee. He'll bring 'em over."

Steve was waiting outside when Lee's truck pulled into the driveway. He opened the top of the cloth bag that lay on the seat beside Lee and pulled out the five pieces, leaving behind the pages of notes Shawn had put with them. "We hafta get these things inside right away."

Lee's curiosity wasn't yet answered, but he was eager to help with whatever was going on. They scurried into the house.

With the five wedges laid out in the circular pie-shaped pattern, Steve explained that Shawn knew much more about the pieces than he did, but he knew there was some significance to that particular arrangement. Peters produced a small camera and began snapping at least a dozen shots of the unusual items from all different angles. Everyone in the room was mesmerized, as they stared, poked, prodded, rubbed, and even sniffed at the mysterious oddities.

Sorenson broke the spell. "The important thing now is to get these things to the airport locker." He turned to Peters and they began discussing whom they might call on to assist with the delivery. Time was running short; they had to make some quick decisions.

"I want to do it," Steve said in a voice loud enough to dominate the chatter.

The agents stopped talking; everyone in the room stared toward Steve in disbelief. Objections immediately sprang up.

"It's too dangerous," Kathy said.

"We don't know who we're dealing with," Don added.

"You could get hurt."

But Steve was persistent. He thought it would make him feel better if he could play an important role in rescuing Shawn.

Leaning on the back of a chair, Sorenson was just listening to all the comments, and half squinting. "Actually, that's not a bad idea..."

Everyone stopped to listen.

"The kidnapper stated an exact time of nine o'clock tonight for the delivery to be made. That means he will be watching from somewhere close by. He's instructed the delivery person to drop the key in a nearby ashtray, and then disappear. I don't think Steve will be in any danger. Now as long as he sees who is making the delivery -- Shawn's young friend -- he will be less suspicious of police involvement, and maybe will drop his guard, feeling less inhibited to recover the package. I can have a dozen or more agents within the immediate area. We shouldn't have any trouble collaring this guy when he makes his move."

Don expressed his concern of Shawn's safety. "But what about Shawn? If you grab this guy--"

Sorenson spoke again with confidence. "The kidnapper is not acting alone. The first note referred to "we." Shawn will not have been left unguarded. We'll be able to find Shawn once we have at least one of them in custody. Worst-case scenario? The co-conspirator will release Shawn at the prescribed time, three a.m., and escape before we get to him. One way or another, I'm quite certain Shawn will be freed and safe. My guess is the kingpin of the operation has a flight booked sometime between nine and midnight. He's probably quite confident he'll be long gone by the time Shawn is released. With a little shrewd planning, we can prevent him from boarding that plane."

Agent Bill Sorenson was one of the best profilers the FBI had. He had gotten inside the head of a man he never met, and his assumptions of the perpatrators' scheme were quite accurate, with minor exceptions. He knew the man he sought was intelligent, but he had to stay one step ahead.

The countdown had begun. They had three and a half hours to prepare. Four o'clock was the very latest Steve and Lee could depart in order to reach the airport with time to spare. As Don and Kathy packed the artifacts into the box, Sorenson marked out on a map the exact route to take the boys to the airport. He was familiar enough with that facility to give accurate instructions regarding parking and entrances into the terminal. The only thing he couldn't provide was the exact location of locker number 337A. Steve would have to hunt for that on his own. Over and over, they went through the entire sequence, step by step. Steve thought the plan was pretty simple, but Sorenson wanted to be absolutely sure that every detail was clearly understood. The terminal, at that time on a Friday night would be crowded and busy, and maybe confusing; there would be little room for error.

Mr. and Mrs. Kelly were to remain at their home. Agent Peters would stay with them, while Sorenson would leave a short time after the boys, taking a different route, in the event anyone was watching them. That probability was slight, but it wasn't worth chancing.

Peters continued the coordination efforts with fellow agents via the phone. There would be a command center set up, and plenty of personnel inside the terminal long before Steve and Lee arrived. Agents would be stationed outside the terminal in cars ready to give chase, if need be. The stage was set, and it was nearly curtain time.

With a full tank of gas, a brand new pack of Marlboros, and a small, taped up cardboard box sitting on the seat between them, Lee pointed his Dodge truck heading west out of town. It was 4:05.

Agent Jeffrey Jarrett, commonly known as "J.J." to fellow agents, had been posted at the lumberyard office. At 4:15, his black Ford sedan stopped in the Kelly driveway. Within seconds, Sorenson was sitting in the passenger seat, and a few seconds later, they were speeding away from the Kelly house.

"J.J.? This is a strange case. Just about the time I think it's getting too easy, ten more things pop into my head." Sorenson picked up the car phone and began dialing a number. "Hello... this is Agent Sorenson... we're in route to Minneapolis... ETA is approximately three hours. Now there's some research I need done right away. I want someone there to compile a list of all the known rare art collectors around the Twin Cities area... might as well include museum managers and private gallery owners, too. Then I want you to get a list of all passengers scheduled to depart Minneapolis International tonight after nine p.m. See if you can match up any names on the two lists. Also check with the Defense Department and any other government agencies that would have *anything* to do with national security. See if anyone is missing five wedge-shaped objects with some sort of coded stuff etched on them." He paused listening to the voice on the other end, then responded. "I don't *know* what these things are. If I knew that, maybe I wouldn't be so concerned that we have only four and a half hours before they might slip away from us. Now get on it... and let me know immediately if you hit on anything."

****

After 100 miles, Steve and Lee had brought up just about every subject they could think of to talk about, but they always reverted back to the present mission, and wondered if Shawn was okay. Steve had many times, in his mind's eye, rehearsed his role, only imagining how the airport terminal would appear. He looked down at the floor of the truck. At his feet was the bag that once held the five wedges. He remembered that all of Shawn's notes were still in it, and he dug them out. "I sure wonder what all this stuff means." Then it hit him; he saw the W. Taylor and the phone number in the margin of one of the pages. "Taylor," he shouted out, startling Lee. "The guy's name is Taylor. And we know how to find him!" He shuffled through the pages some more. Unable to find any additional information, he turned to Lee. "Well at least we have his phone number."

Lee laughed. "What are ya gonna do? Call him and ask for directions to his house?"

"No. I'll give this to one of the FBI agents at the airport. *They'll* know how to find him."

Lee reminded him of Sorenson's strict instructions: under no circumstances were they to talk to anyone at the airport. And all the FBI agents would appear as tourists, or as traveling businessmen. He wouldn't recognize any of them.

Steve thought a minute. "Well, I'll recognize Sorenson. He'll be there. I don't know, but I'll figure out something." He got out the map and studied it to make sure they were on course.

The directions had been easy to follow. By 8:15 they were crossing the Mendota Bridge, only a couple of miles from the airport, and within a few minutes they circled the huge parking lot, finally coming to rest about fifty yards from the main entrance of the terminal. Steve looked at his watch. He had a half hour to kill.

****

Eleven agents, rigged with well-concealed two-way radios so they could communicate with each other at any time, were mingled among the clamorous, bustling throng of weekend travelers. Each one had taken up his assigned position, strategically located so every possible direction was covered. Sorenson and J.J. manned the command center set up in the Airport Security Office. J.J. sat on a stool in front of an array of radio equipment and telephones, monitoring not only their own communications, but also the transmissions of Airport Security and the local police, while Sorenson stood at a window overlooking the main terminal arena, carefully watching for suspicious movements within the crowd.

Another man, Tommy Abbott, had infiltrated the busy terminal. He, too, was keeping his presence unnoticeable -- just another face in the crowd.

Steve nervously looked at his watch; it was ten minutes to nine. "Well... guess it's time I should head in there." He plucked the box off the seat, double-checked his pocket for the key and the quarters he would need to open the locker. "I'll be back in a few minutes." His mind flashed back to the night when he heard Shawn say those same exact words leaning out the library window. Only this time, he would be leaving behind the treasure they had retrieved that night.

Lee was to stay outside in the truck while Steve made the drop. Sorenson had been quite clear: he didn't want more than one of them to come inside. There was no reason to add to the possible risk factor. As soon as Steve had deposited the box in the locker, he was to exit the building quickly, return to Lee's truck, and they were to then begin their trip back to Westland.

With the box clutched under one arm, Steve calmly walked through the main entrance. Sorenson spotted him right away and alerted the other agents. "Everybody get ready to dance -- the band just entered the auditorium."

Steve had two targets in mind: the lockers, and Sorenson. As he wandered through the maze of people, the terminal grew to intimidation. Becoming conscious now of the precarious circumstances surrounding him, he felt a chill tickle at the back of his neck. Steve had never been too fearful of any situation, but as he glanced into the eyes of one stranger after another passing by, he realized how insignificant a single person can be in a crowd, and how easily one lone person could be lost. Certainly there were a dozen or more pairs of eyes watching his every move; certainly he would be protected should danger threaten.

He soon found himself passing by a bank of freestanding lockers, but all those had numbers in the 100's. He kept walking, periodically glancing around to see if anyone was watching or following him, but it seemed that no one was paying any attention to him at all. Then he observed another row of lockers against a wall. As he approached them, he knew he had found his destination, as these all had 300 numbers, but just beyond them, the familiar Agent Sorenson was casually standing in front of a doorway. This was his opportunity to deliver the phone number. He started to make his approach, ready to hand over the small slip of paper; Sorenson made brief eye contact with Steve, shook his head as if to show disgust, turned, and abruptly disappeared through the door, closing it quickly behind him. Steve realized that Sorenson had been dead serious about not making contact with *anyone*. Frustrated, he returned to the lockers and decided that maybe he ought to stick with the choreography that had been so precisely planned.

He stood motionless for a few seconds staring at the number tag 337A, feeling like he was about to sell his soul to the devil by depositing the box that contained his best friend's prized treasure. He slowly reached up, slipped the two quarters into the coin slot, turned the key and pulled the door open. Gently, he set the box inside the locker, closed the door, and put his hand holding the key in his pocket. At the far end of a row of chairs directly behind him, was the floor-stand ashtray, just as the instructions had indicated. At the near end, an elderly couple occupied two of the chairs with suitcases on the floor at their feet. Steve stared at the old man, then at the woman beside him. But neither of them paid the slightest bit of attention as they went on with their conversation. He focused on the ashtray and cautiously started walking toward it, pulling his hand out of his pocket. Pausing only long enough to drop the key in the sand-filled receptacle, he resumed his pace. Ten steps away, he looked over his shoulder to see if anyone was attempting to retrieve the key. It was at that moment he noticed his heart pounding. His only objective now was to find the exit; he didn't want to be anywhere near when locker number 337A was opened.

Only fifteen minutes had ticked away when he jumped back into the truck. Lee asked, "How'd it go?"

"Piece o' cake." Steve struggled to hide his emotion. His heart was still running the Kentucky Derby. "But Sorenson ignored me. I didn't get the phone number to him."

"So what d'ya think we should do now?"

"We've gotta find a phone book. I'll get the address to this phone number, and that's probably where Shawn is."

"Shouldn't we let the cops handle this?"

"They're pretty busy right now... c'mon, let's go find Shawn." Although his whole body displayed tension and worry, Steve smiled inside; he had all but lost control of the treacherous game in which he and Shawn scored the leading points before the kidnapping occurred. But now he had the ball again, and it was time to make a power play. The opposition wouldn't be expecting a sneak attack.

Lee remembered a Texaco service station just down the road from the airport. There would certainly be a telephone directory there.

****

"Subject is approaching the ash tray... he's picking up the key... he's looking toward the locker... he's putting the key in his pocket... he's walking away." One of the nearby agents gave the play-by-play report quietly over the two-way. "Subject is a Caucasian male, about twenty-five, six feet, hundred eighty pounds, dark hair, dark blue shirt, tan pants."

The man being described to all the agents didn't fit the profile. Sorenson was quite sure this was not their prime suspect, but rather just a messenger, and advised the team of agents not to move in on the key bearer just yet. As long as he did not approach the locker, they were only to observe him, and follow him only if he left the terminal. Some of the agents changed their location to better vantage points; one of them was only ten feet away from the phone booth where the messenger dialed a number, but hung up almost right away without conducting any conversation.

"That was probably a signal," Sorenson reported calmly. "Everybody just sit tight... the rooster is bound to get into the hen house any time now."

The mention of the five strange wedges had not set off any bells or whistles with any other government agencies, nor had anything turned up on the national network of stolen goods files. The significance of the objects still wasn't clear in anybody's mind. For right now, Sorenson and his troupe were more concerned about preventing the mastermind of abduction to escape. They were convinced that the kidnapper would attempt to flee the area, and probably the continent, via this airport, and they were determined to avert that occurrence.

Although Sorenson was certain the abductor would use an alias to book travel arrangements, he continued to scan the list of known dealers and collectors, comparing it to the airlines' passenger lists in hopes of stumbling across something positive. He had it well within his power to suspend any flights from departure, but that would only cause alarm and scare off the guilty party; that would have to be a last-minute effort to implement an otherwise failed capture. A young boy's life was in the balance; Sorenson recalled past cases when one wrong move meant the difference between winning and losing. He thought about the devastation on the faces of family when he had lost. He envisioned Mr. and Mrs. Kelly sitting at their kitchen table, terrified, anxious, and helpless.

"J.J.," he said. "Phone the Kellys. Let them know everything is proceeding smoothly as planned and that Steve and Lee are on their way back to Westland."

****

"There must be a thousand Taylors listed here." Steve studied the phone book that could easily qualify as weightlifting equipment, while Lee instructed the attendant to fill the gas tank. He remembered the initials; at least he had it narrowed down to a first name starting with W, and carefully looked at each entry. Finally, he spotted a match. "Here it is. One with the same number." He wrote down the address and sprinted to the station attendant who had just finished filling the tank.

"Can you tell us how to find 2020 Riverview Terrace?"

****

Shawn had nearly finished the plate of spaghetti and meatballs when Taylor sat down. "I'm sure you will be pleased to hear that tonight will be your last night as my guest. I have just received the signal from my associate that the artifacts have been delivered."

Shawn stared blankly at his adversary, trying to hide his emotions.

"I will be leaving shortly," Taylor continued. "But Tommy and Curtis will take care of you. At three a.m. they will escort you out. Please cooperate with them, and by the way..." A sneer hung on his face, and he spoke his final words as one last attempt at intimidation. "I hope you have had plenty of time to think about your future at the University."

In one respect, Shawn was disappointed that Steve had actually given up the artifacts; they were probably gone forever. On the other hand, it did mean he was going to be out of this confinement and breathing fresh air by morning, and that was a welcomed thought. He had been reduced to nothing more than helpless, and he was ready to concede to defeat, now that Taylor seemed to have the upper hand. Shawn could only hope that Taylor had enough decency to fulfill his promise, even if it meant another long ride locked in the trunk of a car.

CHAPTER 15

Lee pulled up to the curb and stopped next to a six-foot-high stone wall surrounding the perimeter of the huge lawn and gardens of the structure that, to Steve and Lee, looked more like a castle. A wrought iron gate with 2020 on it blocked the entrance to the long driveway. This *had* to be the place, and it appeared as though their only way in would be over the rock wall. Scaling the barrier seemed a simple task compared to finding Shawn, if he was there at all.

Ducking behind bushes and trees, and taking advantage of near darkness and every shadow as cover, they zigzagged their way to the unattached garage about fifty feet from the house. Peeking around the corner, they could see light coming from only a couple of windows on the ground floor. The walk-in garage door was open, and it seemed to be a good opportunity to get out of sight. The interior of the building was dark, but the flame from Steve's cigarette lighter provided enough light to see the black Mercedes sedan on the far side of the otherwise empty garage.

Steve spotted something shiny on the floor; it was Shawn's keys. He recognized the Mustang key ring -- the one he had given Shawn as a birthday gift. Now he knew Shawn must be somewhere in that mansion. He slipped the keys into his pocket, and once again, under the cover of the shadows, they snuck to a window, not far from the front door. Curtains prevented them from seeing into the lighted room, but the window was open slightly, and Steve recognized one of the voices he heard: "Tommy will return from the airport a half hour after I leave here. The two of you will dispose of Mr. Kelly. But you must wait until three o'clock. I should be landing in New York by that time. He will cooperate with you... he thinks he is going home. As soon as you have accomplished that, return here at once and begin loading all my precious art into the U-Haul truck. When you arrive in Miami, this is the phone number to call. My associate there will meet you and take you to his warehouse."

On the edge of panic, Steve put what he had just heard into reasonable perspective. Anyone would have drawn the same conclusion under these circumstances. "They're going to kill Shawn!" he whispered to Lee. "We've got until three o'clock to get him out of there!"

The front door, not more than fifteen feet away, swung open, and out stepped a gray-haired man that Steve had seen before only in darkness. Lee had seen him, too, but with blackened eyes and bandages. They ducked down behind the shrubbery; Taylor stopped and peered toward them, as if he had noticed their presence. Steve feared they had been caught, but he had the presence of mind to hold his breath and not move a muscle. He was thankful that Lee did the same. Taylor turned and stepped back toward the door, opened it again and called out, "Curtis? Make sure this front window gets closed and locked."

"Yes sir, I'll do it right away," a distant voice returned.

Taylor walked to the garage. A few minutes later, the overhead garage door opened; the black Mercedes emerged and sped down the driveway.

"Get away from this window," Steve whispered. He nudged Lee and pointed. They had barely cleared the next shrub when the open window slammed shut behind them.

The landscape dropped off to a lower level at the rear of the house. More trees back there cast more shadows, and by then dusk had faded to total black; concealment seemed less of a problem. Steve and Lee crouched in the shadows and surveyed the possibilities.

A large wooden deck jutted out from the house; dim light shone from sliding glass doors. As the rest of the windows all appeared dark, it seemed safe to assume that whoever was in there occupied the room just inside the glass doors, but no movement could be detected so there was no way to be absolutely sure.

"D'ya think Shawn is in there?" Lee whispered.

"Don't know," Steve responded. "But we gotta figure a way to find out."

"Got any ideas?"

"Yeah." Steve thought a moment, and then instructed Lee. "I'll hide behind the bushes next to the door. Then you make some noise out here, and stay outa sight. When the guy comes out, I'll jump him from behind."

"That might work," Lee said.

"It's gotta work. We don't have much time."

With the stealth of a cat on a hunt, Steve took his position at the shrubs by the door; he searched the darkness for Lee, but Lee was definitely well camouflaged in the shadows. He readied himself to spring into action. They would have but one chance to make the strike – *they could not fail*.

In the still, dark night, two wrought iron patio chairs clanging together rang out like the head-on collision of two freight trains. Steve thought *a little noise* would do, but this would probably alert the whole neighborhood.

He couldn't see the glass door, but he could hear it slide open. His entire body tensed preparing for the attack.

A shirtless, sinewy mountain of masculinity, half again Steve's size, strolled out to the edge of the patio. Steve knew he was in trouble. But Shawn's life was on the line, and there might not be another opportunity with this advantage. Just as Steve made a lunge, his unsuspecting opponent turned. Curtis' reaction was like lightning as he planted a fist solidly into Steve's chest, knocking him down to a sitting position on the patio floor. The hulk just stood there with clenched fists, anticipating Steve's next move. Steve realized it was wiser to sit motionless, at least long enough to give Lee time to arrive and even out the odds a little. Then, from out of the darkness he saw the chair come flying – another train collision – this time the patio chair squarely making contact with the back of hulk's head. He fell to the floor, moaned, and went limp.

Lee stood holding the chair, looking down at the body sprawled out at his feet. "You okay, Allison?"

"Better than *he* is. *Good shot!*" Steve was moderately dazzled by Lee's performance, but quite thankful for the outcome of the predicament.

Not knowing if there was anyone else in the house, they quietly snuck through the open doorway into the dimly lit expanse, listening for any other activity. Shawn had to be there, somewhere; little time remained before the other person Taylor had mentioned would return, and maybe the guy they had just laid out cold on the patio would wake up -- he definitely wouldn't be in a good mood. There was no time to waste.

In a screaming whisper, Steve called out. "*Sherlock... are you here?*" He glanced around the room filled with armless statues, antique furniture and a polished suit of armor standing sentry under an arch at the head of a long hallway.

In the locked room just down the hall, Shawn barely heard the summons. He noticed the earlier commotion and had turned off the record player. Once again, and more clearly this time, he heard the loud whisper. *"Sherlock... where are you?"* There was only one person who called him "Sherlock," he thought, but what was *Steve* doing there?

"I'm in here!" he said excitedly and hammered on the door with clenched fists. Steve followed the pounding sound to the locked door. "We've gotta get you outa here... they're gonna *kill you!*"

Shawn's excitement elevated at a rapid pace. *"Get the damn door open!"*

"It's locked. Where's the key?"

"How the hell should I know? I'm the captive here... remember?"

Steve threw his body weight, shoulder-first against the door several times with no results. Surely, if anyone else were in the house, they would have heard this disturbance and would have been there by now. Steve's adrenalin was pumping. He looked around, and returned seconds later with a heavy wooden chair. Grabbing the chair at the top of the backrest, he hurtled it against the door in a roundhouse swing. The chair disintegrated, sending broken splinters flying in all directions. The door didn't budge.

Lee calmly approached as Steve stood there in bewilderment, staring at the unmovable barrier. "I found these keys in that guy's pocket," he said. He slipped a key into the lock, turned the knob and swung the door open.

Shawn stood four feet back from the doorway with a look of total astonishment. He stepped forward toward Steve; they threw their arms around one another in a long, hard hug, their heads pressed tightly together.

"I was afraid I'd never see you again," Steve whispered, fighting back the tears.

Shawn just stood there embracing his best friend for a few seconds, and then spoke softly. "Happy Birthday... dear Watson."

"I hate to break up the party," Lee broke in with urgency. "But can you save this for later? *We need to get outa here!"*

They headed for the patio door, each hopping over the motionless body lying just outside.

"Wow! What happened to Curtis?" Shawn quizzed.

"He ran into a chair. I'll explain later," Steve replied as they darted into the shadows around the corner. A Dodge pickup truck and freedom was just over the rock wall.

****

"A local police patrolman called in a Wisconsin license plate number a few minutes ago from a *Beverley Hills* type neighborhood," J.J. reported to Sorenson the radio transmissions he had just monitored. "The number just came back registered to a Dodge truck owned by Lee Krueger from Westland. Isn't that the driver who brought Allison here?"

"That's right." Sorenson never broke his stare fixed on the locker area through the half-opened door. "What are they doing?"

"The truck's abandoned. And it's kind of an unusual vehicle for that neighborhood this time of night -- that's what caught their attention."

"Maybe they got lost on their way out of town, and ran out of gas or something." Sorenson pondered on that a few moments, recalling Steve's attempt to make contact with him during the ransom drop. "Maybe you ought to send somebody over there, just in case."

"The locals already dispatched a back-up, but I'll get one of our guys on the way too."

Eleven pairs of eyes inconspicuously fixed on Tommy Abbott, who still had the key for locker 337A in his pocket. So far, he had made no physical contact with anyone or executed any suspicious moves; he just sat quietly drinking his coffee and scanning the pages of a newspaper. It was difficult to determine if anyone else among the multitude of strange faces milling about watched him, or were preparing to make an advance toward him. Sorenson knew they were fast approaching a critical, time sensitive event; passenger boarding instructions for Flight 214 to New York had already been announced over the public address speakers. One false move, one miscalculated action or the slightest wrong judgment could spell failure of their strategy, and even worse, catastrophe for Shawn Kelly.

Several minutes ticked by. The messenger frequently glanced at his wristwatch; his nervousness escalated. Something was about to happen. The agents prepared mentally, anticipating a skirmish. Well trained in surveillance, pursuit, and hand-to-hand combat, they were ready for anything.

Folding the newspaper, the messenger tossed it on the table, abruptly stood, and began walking, slowly at first, and then quickened his pace, merging with a group of suitcase-toting travelers hurrying toward the taxi stand.

"He's on the move... he's headed for the main entrance," the agent with the best vantage point reported to the others. The rest of the agents started moving in the same direction. Sorenson radioed his instructions: "Let him get clear of the building before you make the hit... we don't want a bunch of innocent by-standers getting hurt... and whatever you do, *don't* let him get out of the parking lot."

Pedestrian traffic had increased. Two arriving flights were staging at gates four and six. There was only one departure scheduled within the next twenty minutes. Sorenson looked at the clock. "Get ready to have the tower hold Flight 214 to New York -- but not 'til you hear my command."

In all the confusion of the heavy pedestrian movement through and around the main entrance, none of the agents noticed the brush-by hand-off of the key to Taylor as he met Tommy amidst the crowded passageway. They were concentrating their attention to the man they had been watching since 9:00 and didn't realize the prime target was walking right past them. Once Tommy reached the black Mercedes, six agents converged and wrestled him to the ground.

Something seemed wrong to Sorenson. "Okay... call the tower." He exited the office to get closer to the locker area. If his earlier hunch was correct, and the kidnapper *was* using mass confusion as cover, this would be the perfect time to make the pick-up, when there were more people moving about. And now there were no other agents watching this area; all the attention had been drawn to the main entrance. To the best of his knowledge, the messenger still had possession of the key, but there also existed the possibility something could have been missed.

Even Sorenson almost missed seeing the smartly dressed, gray-haired man drop the quarters into the slot of locker 337A. Taylor inserted the key, gave it a turn, and opened the door. As he stared into the empty compartment, a shiny handcuff snapped around his wrist. "FBI – *you're mine,"* Sorenson said as he, too, stared curiously into the empty locker. Within seconds, he had both of Taylor's hands secured, and began forcibly walking the less-than-cooperative criminal toward the Security Office, where he sat the gray-haired man on a chair. "You're under arrest for abduction and extortion. You have the right to remain silent..."

When Sorenson had finished reading the Miranda, he reached inside Taylor's sport jacket and pulled out the boarding pass. "Looks like there's going to be one vacant seat on Flight 214 tonight, Mr..... Deveron."

Just as Sorenson had suspected, Taylor purchased the ticket under an assumed name. A wallet in the same pocket containing a driver's license and credit cards revealed his true identity. As he stared at the address on the license, Sorenson realized now that Steve and Lee might be getting themselves into a dangerous situation. He grabbed Taylor's lapel, nearly hoisting him out of the chair. "Where are you holding Shawn Kelly?" he demanded.

Taylor said nothing.

"If you've harmed one hair on that boy's head, I'll personally kick your ass into next week. Now *where is he?"*

"I don't know what you're talking about," Taylor answered.

"J.J. -- has anyone been sent to Krueger's abandoned truck yet?"

"Not yet. We all had our hands full."

"Well get over there right away! I think you're going to find it at 2020 Riverview Terrace... that's where Shawn Kelly is probably being held... and I'm afraid his friends might be trying to rescue him."

Woodrow Taylor wasn't answering any of Sorenson's questions; he only demanded his lawyer's presence. And Tommy Abbott, in another room, was producing the same negative results. Obviously, Shawn's whereabouts would not be learned from either of them. Sorenson could only hope that his speculation was correct, and that his men could arrive at the forbidding scene prior to it evolving a deadly one. The airport crisis was over, but another still remained at 2020 Riverview Terrace.

With J.J. competently in command of the rescue team dispatched to the

Taylor residence, Sorenson quickly recruited the assistance of three other agents, and transported Taylor and Abbot to the Hennepin County Jail. There, in a controlled and protected environment, they continued their thorough investigation.

****

Lee's truck was just beyond the stone wall about thirty yards past the front of the house. As Steve had it figured, Taylor's other assistant would be returning soon; he spoke to Shawn quickly and to the point: "Follow me."

"Where are we?" Shawn asked.

"St. Paul."

"But how did you find me?"

"It's a long story... I'll tell you later."

They sprinted through the shadows toward their freedom, but this time the darkness played to their disadvantage; at first, Steve thought it was Taylor's henchmen tackling him from behind; Shawn didn't have time to draw any conclusions; Lee turned just in time to see the uniformed police officer grab his arm. He struggled to get free, but a second uniform pounced on him and wrestled him to the ground. Handcuffs were on their wrists before they had the time to even think about what was happening. It seemed useless to resist.

From the chatter among the officers and the radio transmission one of them made with a walkie-talkie, Shawn quickly realized the policemen had considered them burglars. In desperation he tried to explain. "You've made a mistake! I was kidnapped and my friends just rescued me!"

Steve joined the protest. "You'll find one of the *real* culprits unconscious on the back patio."

The cops hoisted them to their feet. "Kidnapped, were you?" one of the cops said sarcastically. "That's a good one. You can tell that to the Arraignment Judge on Monday."

With an undue degree of roughness, the four policemen forced the boys to walk toward the gate where a pair of black-and-white squad cars waited. The officers were convinced they had just captured burglars, and that didn't seem anything out-of-the-ordinary. The FBI had kept the information about the abduction and the airport surveillance operation to themselves for security reasons; the local police had no reason to believe this wasn't just a routine burglary.

"But I really was kidnapped," Shawn persisted.

"He's telling the truth," Steve added.

The pleas were rudely ignored as the officers conducted their routine pat-down search for concealed weapons and then stuffed the boys into the rear seat of the squad car. They had heard a lot of excuses from trespassers before, and this one seemed a little far-fetched.

As the paddy wagon whisked the alleged housebreakers to a precinct station, three more back-up cars arrived. With weapons drawn, eight uniformed officers began a search of the premises.

They had determined there were no other occupants or intruders in the house; no signs of forced entry -- only an open patio door at the rear of the house, and the only unusual element was a broken-up chair in the lower level. By the time Agent Jarrett arrived, they were gathered once again near the front door.

J.J. held up his I.D. and badge. "Agent Jarrett--FBI." He asked for particulars.

Reluctantly, the senior officer reported, "Just a simple, routine house burglary. Everything's under control. The suspects are already in custody. I don't think we need the FBI's help on this one."

"Suspects?" J.J. returned with alarm. "Two boys about 18 years old?"

"Three, actually. Why?"

"This wasn't just a routine burglary," J.J. snapped. "Is there anyone else in the house?"

By the tone of Agent Jarrett's voice, the local cops became curious. "No… there's no one in the house."

"Are you absolutely certain of that?"

"Yes, absolutely. What's this all about?"

"One of the boys you just apprehended is a kidnap victim. He was being held hostage in this house. Where is he now?"

"All three were taken to our precinct lock-up."

Three more plain sedans came to a screeching stop at the end of the driveway; eight more FBI agents swarmed to the muster. J.J. began firing orders in rapid succession: "Seal off the entire area; *no one* enters or leaves these premises; make a room-by-room search of the house for anyone that might still be there; we're dealing with kidnappers and extortionists, so I don't want any negligence in preserving every scrap of evidence; I want written statements from all the local officers…"

With the commands delivered, the G-men hustled off to their assigned duties. Jarrett zeroed in on the Uniform who seemed to be the spokesman for the local platoon: "The three boys you arrested… were they all okay? Were any of them injured?"

"Well, they didn't put up much of a fight, but they seemed to be in good health."

"Did they say anything?"

"Only the one… the smallest one of the three… kept yappin' about being kidnapped."

"And you didn't question that?"

"Look. When you're dealin' with a bunch of young hoodlums, you hear a lot of crazy stuff—"

"Never mind. Take me to your precinct station."

****

The Desk Sergeant produced three large brown envelopes containing the confiscated billfolds, keys, loose change, cigarette lighters, and from the one marked *Steven Allison*, a slip of paper with a phone number and Taylor's address. J.J. opened each wallet and examined the identification, paying little attention to any other items. "I hope you guys are proud of yourselves. You've just arrested a kidnapping victim and his two friends... who probably rescued him."

The Sergeant just pressed his lips together, shook his head slowly, and said nothing.

Jarrett picked the keys from Lee Krueger's belongings and dangled them in front of the Sergeant. "These are the keys for the pickup truck at the scene. Have it brought here right away. Now where are the boys?"

The red-faced Sergeant took the keys from J.J. and directed him down a hallway to an interrogation room where Shawn, Steve and Lee sat, still handcuffed. He had never met any of them face-to-face, but he recognized Shawn from a photograph Sorenson obtained from the Kellys, and Steve, from the brief encounter at the airport.

"Get those cuffs off them," Jarrett ordered the uniformed guard at the doorway. "Give them back their belongings," he directed the Sergeant, "and get them to a phone. I'm sure they want to call their homes. Then put us someplace a little more comfortable, where we can talk."

Agent Jarrett raised a few eyebrows and caused a number of frowns among the men in blue; the arrests had been swiftly nullified.

He introduced himself to the boys while the Sergeant returned their personal effects.

It was nearly midnight when Shawn dialed the phone. "Hello, Mom?"

"Shawn! It's really you! Where are you? Are you okay?"

He could hear the teardrops in his mother's voice. "Yes, Mom. I'm fine. I'm at a Police Station now, and Steve and Lee are here too."

Choked with emotion, Kathy Kelly could speak no more; she handed the receiver to Don to finish the conversation. Richard Allison, John and Lucy Krueger were all at the Kelly house, too, offering their support, and anxiously awaiting their sons' return; they all took their turns, talking with the boys. Although the parents weren't aware of the added danger the boys had created, the relief was overwhelming.

When they were finished, J.J. took the phone and requested to speak with Don Kelly: "This is Agent Jarrett, FBI. I know you're anxious for Shawn to return home, but as you might guess, we have a lot of questions that need answers right away."

"I understand."

"We have the kidnappers in custody."

"That's good to know. Shawn said he's okay. Is he okay?"

"Yes, Mr. Kelly, Shawn is fine. I just wanted to tell you that he and the others will be here with us several more hours yet."

"Should we come there to pick him up?"

"I don't think that will be necessary. I've already offered them a motel room when we're finished, but they've indicated to me that they just want to go home. Lee Krueger seems quite alert and able to drive back to Westland."

J.J. politely wrapped up the conversation by asking to speak with Agent Peters, diligently standing by at the Kelly residence. "You can pack up now, Terry. We've got the boy, and the suspects are in custody…"

He hung up the phone and immediately started jotting some notes. Shawn, Steve and Lee stared eagerly across the table at the man who had rescued them from the depths of misunderstanding, but then their zeal melted away as Jarrett skewered Steve and Lee with a stern, condescending glare. "That was a pretty dumb stunt you pulled, going in there alone. You could've gotten yourselves killed."

Steve hung his head; frustration oozed from every pore. He had tried to alert Sorenson at the airport terminal, but was ignored, and now he was being rewarded with a reprimand for what he thought was a heroic deed.

"But I gotta hand it to ya," J.J. continued. "You should be commended for your bravery."

Steve blushed. Lee half grinned.

Jarrett turned to Shawn. "You're lucky to have such loyal friends."

Shawn laid his hand on Steve's shoulder. Truer words did not exist.

"Good thing, too, that there was no one else in the house to stop you," J.J. said.

"But there *was* someone else there," Lee piped up.

"Yeah," Shawn added. "Curtis was there."

"Curtis? Who is Curtis?" J.J. asked.

"One of Taylor's goons," Shawn answered.

"Lee clobbered him with a lawn chair," Steve explained. "He was still laid out cold on the back patio when we left there."

They described Curtis; Shawn explained that Curtis was one of two men who had stuffed him into the trunk of a car at the lake, and that he had shared the guard duty at the mansion with the other man named Tommy. Steve and Lee told Jarrett how they had discovered the third man's presence and had lured him out onto the patio, and about their confrontation with him.

J.J. quickly realized, now, that the third person involved in the kidnapping must still be at large; the man they called Curtis had escaped.

"Are you sure he was still there when you left the house?"

"We tripped over him coming out."

Jarrett's fingers danced on the phone dial; he relayed the information about Curtis to the investigators stationed at the Taylor house, dialed another number and recited the same message to Sorenson. When he finished, he turned to Shawn. "Okay. We've got a lot to cover. Let's start at the beginning."

They recreated the chain of events from the abduction at the lake, to being handcuffed at the Taylor residence. Jarrett possessed that quality that wouldn't let a single detail escape without notice, without scrutiny, without complete documentation. He had a job to do: to learn and communicate Shawn's entire story with accuracy, as if he had lived it himself.

Four hours later, Jarrett was satisfied he had accumulated enough information, and once again offered to provide motel rooms for them, but the boys declined.

"I want to go home," Shawn insisted. Steve and Lee agreed.

"Okay," J.J. said. "Guess I don't blame you for that. I had Lee's truck brought here; it should be waiting for you outside."

He escorted the boys into the parking lot. "There's going to be more questions later," J.J. said as they walked.

Shawn nodded. He couldn't imagine any questions that J.J.'s thoroughness had missed. Jarrett had even called in an artist to create a composite sketch of Curtis. But inquiries regarding his knowledge of the artifacts had been minimal, and Shawn was glad to avoid the subject.

Jarrett's rigid temperament had remained persistent all night, but a little compassion finally broke through. "Are you sure you'll be alright to drive home?"

"Sure, I'll be fine," Lee replied.

"Can you find the right road?"

"We still have the map... we're okay... really," Steve added.

J.J. still seemed concerned. "Well, if you have any problems--"

"We'll be fine."

Jarrett drove away toward the Taylor mansion. He wanted to verify some of the details Shawn had given in his statement and check on the investigation's progress. Then he would join Sorenson at the county jail, and start preparing his reports.

Lee found the highway easily, and pointed his truck homeward bound. He thought the episode was over; he was tired, and he was eager to see St. Paul in his rear view mirror. Shawn was exhausted, too. He leaned back in the seat and closed his eyes. "If you get too tired, I'll drive for a while," he said to Lee.

They had only gone a couple of miles when Steve made an abrupt announcement: "Stop! Turn around. We have to go back to the airport."

"Why?" Lee asked.

Steve wasn't sure he would find what he was looking for, and he didn't want to falsely raise any hopes. But after all they had been through he had to try. "I... I want to pick up... a souvenir."

Lee thought Steve had lost his mind for sure, but gave in to his request and drove back to the airport. Steve darted into the terminal while the others waited in the truck. It was much less crowded and busy at 5:30 a.m. And this time, he knew exactly where he was going. Only five minutes later, he came out again. Lee recognized the small cardboard box that Steve carried, but he didn't say anything. Shawn was a bit puzzled.

"This is for you." Steve grinned as he laid the box on Shawn's lap. "But don't open it just yet... not 'til we get away from here."

****

By 6:00 a.m., Sorenson and Jarrett were ready to call it a night; the last few days had allowed little time for sleep, and they were ready to check into the hotel. Taylor and his accomplice were securely incarcerated in the Hennepin County Jail, pages upon pages of reports had been written, and dozens of phone calls made. Everything was complete, except for one last stop at the airport terminal. Sorenson was still puzzled over the vanishing box containing the five artifacts. Perhaps, if he went back to the scene he could better reconstruct in his mind's eye what had taken place.

All accounts had confirmed there was a third person involved in the abduction; Lee had laid him out cold on the patio. Sorenson could only speculate that he must have regained consciousness and had escaped before the police searched the rear of the house after apprehending the boys. The sketch of the man they only knew as Curtis already circulated the entire area.

Sorenson knew he saw Steve put the box in the locker. To him, this had become as much a mystery as the abduction had been in the beginning. He could make all sorts of speculations; but there still didn't seem to be a logical explanation, and now he was beginning to believe that he had been outsmarted -- by an eighteen-year-old kid.

CHAPTER 16

The news about Shawn's abduction and rescue had spread quickly. Cars and vans displaying various news agency, TV and radio station logos lined both sides of the roadway in front of the Kellys' rural home; dozens of reporters were trying to capture the human interest side of the story. This was a monumental event in the quiet little midwestern community, falling on the heels of a fatal hit and run that had not been resolved. But even Sara's death now seemed less significant compared to the kidnapping that had gained immediate national attention.

When Sorenson arrived about noon on Sunday, the mob of reporters flocked around him with microphones, cameras, and a barrage of questions as he made his way to the door.

"Two of the three known kidnappers are in custody," he told them. "The FBI has the incident under intense investigation. Beyond that, I have no further comments at this time." More queries erupted from the curious crowd, but Sorenson would say no more. Kathy Kelly recognized him as she peeked out the window. She opened the door cautiously and Sorenson quickly ducked inside.

"We've practically been prisoners here since early this morning," Kathy said, nearly in tears. "We can't get out of the house without being hounded. We couldn't even go to church... and I finally had to take the phone off the hook."

Sorenson wasn't surprised, but he sympathized with the Kellys' dilemma. "You'll have to face them sooner or later. I'll prep you, Shawn in particular, for a formal press conference later. That might get the reporters off your backs, and out of your front lawn. But right now, my priority is to speak with Shawn, and then I have to locate Steve."

Don informed Sorenson that Steve was already there. "He's stayed here with Shawn since they returned yesterday. They're both up in Shawn's room." He was thinking of Steve with high regard now; he owed Steve Allison an enormous debt of thanks for preventing a tragic ending to the drama they had all endured during the past few days.

Sorenson took from his briefcase nine photographs of men, all having features similar to Woodrow Taylor's. He instructed Shawn to examine the photos carefully, and to point out the man who had held him in captivity. Shawn studied each picture, and without hesitation, he said, "This is him," and confidently handed Taylor's photo to Sorenson. It was a face he had learned to know well.

Sorenson sighed with relief. He inserted the photos in a large envelope, and placed it back in his briefcase. The *victim* had positively identified the *criminal.*

Sorenson turned to Steve. "Now... I saw you put the box in the locker at the airport, but somehow it managed to disappear by the time Taylor got there. My theory is that our third suspect got to it, but we haven't located him or the artifacts...what can you tell me about this guy? You and Shawn are the only ones who have ever seen him."

Steve dug into his pocket. "I was going to keep this for a souvenir," he said as he tossed a key to Sorenson. Shawn's eyes widened. Steve had explained his clever last-second actions to Shawn, and now Shawn was certain the artifacts would finally have to be surrendered.

Steve continued, "That night at the airport, after you ignored me when I tried to tell you where to find Shawn, I stood there looking at the locker, and I noticed the locker next to 337A still had the key in the lock. I figured it wasn't in use, so I opened that one and put the box in it. I switched the keys in my pocket and dropped the 337 key in the ashtray, just like I was supposed to."

Sorenson examined the key stamped 338A.

Steve went on. "I know how important those things are to Shawn, and I figured that was the only way to keep the crooks from getting their hands on 'em... for a while anyway."

Sorenson's face flushed. He realized then, that not he, or any of his men, had been close enough, or at the proper angle to notice the clever locker switch. Apparently, Tommy Abbot had not noticed it, either.

"Have you ever considered a career with the FBI?" Sorenson asked. He thought anyone who could think that fast, in that situation, *must* have some special talents.

He went to the phone, dialed the number to the airport security office, and engaged in a lengthy conversation. There was a long period of silence while he waited for the security officer to locate an extra key for locker 338A and to check its contents. Shawn and Steve sat quietly, exchanging no more than glances. Being such close companions, they had developed a nearly telepathic relationship. They didn't need to speak.

Sorenson returned with a bewildered expression and said, "Well... 338A is empty, too. It seems the artifacts have indeed vanished." He didn't know what had really happened to them, but he couldn't allow that to interfere with his continuing the investigation; there was enough evidence, without the artifacts, to build a solid case against Taylor.

****

By mid-afternoon the reporters were getting restless; the news media had missed the opportunity to report the incident, from the scene, as it happened, because it had been kept under wraps so well. A teenager from a small town had been kidnapped; the story had grown to Titanic-sized proportions, and the news people wanted that story.

Agent Sorenson advised Shawn, his parents, and Steve that facing the reporters and answering a few questions was the only way to get rid of the press army bivouacked on the front lawn. He gave them prepared answers to anticipated questions and warned them about the brutal persistence, against which they would have to defend. "If questions come up regarding the whereabouts of the artifacts, just say that you don't know. And if it gets ugly out there, I'll break it off."

Sorenson stepped out onto the open porch first; a dozen microphones lunged toward him.

"Shawn Kelly, his family, and Steve Allison will answer your questions now. They have suffered an emotionally traumatic experience, so show them some professional courtesy."

Shawn stared at the intimidating microphones and the curious faces behind them, thinking this experience might be worse than the kidnapping had been. Cameras flashed, and for nearly an hour, the reporters fired their questions, most of them directed at Shawn, although, Mr. and Mrs. Kelly answered their share, and Steve was asked to render his version of the rescue.

"Shawn -- were you injured in any way during the ordeal?" one of the reporters blared out.

"Only when I was being rescued. Steve hugged me so hard he knocked the wind out of me." Everyone laughed at the response. "Actually, I owe my life to Steve Allison... everyone should have a friend like him."

Shawn pushed his way back into the house. He'd had enough. Steve quickly followed, and then Don and Kathy disappeared through the doorway as well.

Sorenson convinced the reporters that the conference had ended, and urged them to leave the premises immediately. Only a few lingered briefly, with some last-chance attempts at gaining bits of information, but they soon realized that they would get no more.

CHAPTER 17

At first, Shawn and Steve were flattered by all the attention they received. They had collected enough newspaper clippings to fill a whole scrapbook; their pictures and various accounts of the kidnapping and rescue had been front-page material in just about every major publication in the country, and the front porch press conference film had aired on almost every TV news show. But after two weeks, they only hoped the spotlight would burn out. Their lives had been dramatically affected; they were the center of attention constantly. The library had never seen so much traffic. Shawn couldn't escape his celebrity status at the lumberyard, either, although, Don Kelly was pleased with the increased business it seemed to inspire. Steve's portrayal as a hero by the press had attracted new customers to Edgar's Service Garage, too, and everyone wanted to shake the hero's hand.

But when Shawn and Steve weren't at their jobs, they were seldom apart; they seemed to find all the security they needed in each other. Steve had all but taken up residency at the Kelly home. What once had been less than approval, Don Kelly's negative attitude toward Steve was now firmly replaced with that of admiration; he was seeing the genuine values in Steve that he had completely overlooked in the past, and he and Kathy were now often referring to Steve as their adopted son. He was welcome to stay in their home as long as he wished. There, Steve and Shawn could take advantage of every possible minute until they would be separated for months at a time, when Shawn would be away at college, and they could eat, sleep, and watch TV without being bothered by celebrity seekers. They knew that all those people meant well, but Shawn and Steve were getting tired of the public attention.

There was another motivation for Steve to spend nearly every night at the Kellys.' Richard Allison had been dating Jan Williams, an attractive Westland High English teacher. She was spending more and more time at the Allison home, and the relationship was escalating. Steve was happy for his

Dad's well-deserved social life, and he knew they needed their privacy, too.

Because of the busy work schedule at the garage, and Richard's new romance gaining momentum, Steve rarely spent any time with his father. Kathy Kelly noticed Steve's spirits sinking because of Richard's lack of attention, so she encouraged Richard and Jan to make frequent evening visits. They were a boost to Steve's morale, and Don and Kathy enjoyed the visits, as well. Life was slowly returning to normal in the aftermath.

****

The phone rang one night, interrupting *The Twilight Zone,* one of Steve's favorite TV shows. Shawn detected some urgency in Lee's voice.

"Can you and Allison meet me at the Bowling Alley? I gotta talk to ya."

Shawn and Steve had not seen much of Lee since their return from St. Paul. He hadn't been present during the press conference fiasco, so he had not received nearly as much recognition, even though Steve had attributed him with much of the credit for Shawn's rescue. But seeing what his friends were going through, Lee was glad the limelight was not shining on him too brightly.

Neither Shawn nor Steve were too enthused about making an appearance at the popular gathering spot. Lately, they had been quite successful at avoiding the public, but they respected their friend's seemingly urgent request, and went anyway. It would be good to see Lee again.

When Steve entered the sparsely occupied barroom, he was relieved to see so few people there. He and Shawn acknowledged a few friendly greetings, and then probed for Lee's face. Lee sat alone, near the end of the horseshoe bar; a television, mounted on the wall to his right, was tuned to the ten o'clock news, but Lee wasn't concentrating on the news. His stare was fixed somewhere in the distance, and his expression appeared worried and confused.

"Hi, Lee," Shawn said, and sat down.

"Kelly, Allison." Lee's spirit seemed to come alive when he noticed Steve and Shawn.

"Sorry we haven't been around much, lately," Steve said. "Kinda been stayin' outa sight—"

"Yeah, I know. Don't blame you."

"So, what's been happening with you, Lee?"

"You remember when I told you about my girlfriend that dumped me?" Lee went on to explain about his estranged girlfriend; she had suddenly resurfaced after two months, and she was three months pregnant. There was no doubt that Lee was the father.

Mixed emotions were getting the best of Lee: happy, that he had reunited with his girlfriend; nervous, about being a father; worried, that he wasn't ready for marriage. Lee was seeking the needed support of his best friends.

Their close association with Lee had simply been interrupted, but

Shawn and Steve knew that this couldn't interfere with an esteemed friendship.

"It'll be okay," Shawn said.

"Yeah," Steve reassured, "We'll be here for you."

The TV newscaster had just returned to the air after several commercials. Shawn jerked his head toward the screen when he heard the name *Woodrow Taylor.*

> *"...Taylor, the Minnesota University Professor, mastermind in the abduction of a Westland teen-ager, has now been connected to a world-wide theft ring. Over one million dollars worth of stolen rare paintings and sculptures were recovered from Taylor's St. Paul mansion, where the kidnapped victim was held for three days before his rescue. FBI spokesman, Bill Sorenson, told news reporters that the Bureau had identified the missing art through insurance claims, and that ten other people have been arrested as key players in the thefts. Many more arrests are expected, including Taylor's second accomplice in the kidnapping, who is still at large."*

Steve glanced around the room, discretely trying to determine if others had noticed the newscast. It seemed that no one was paying any attention to it, and he was glad they weren't. Now that the kidnapping story was beginning to cool off, the focus was shifting to new developments, and to Shawn and Steve, that meant another wave of public attention they would rather avoid.

Steve recalled the night of the rescue, and the antique wooden chair he had destroyed. "I wonder how much that chair was worth."

"Well, you'd better start saving," Shawn joked. "The Queen of England will certainly make you pay for it."

CHAPTER 18

There had been little mention of the missing ransom artifacts in any of the papers. Obviously, the FBI had bigger fish to fry. The five wedges had not shown up on any lists of missing artifacts, and they, or the deceased woman who had discovered them, could not be linked to any breach in national security. The Bureau considered the vanished pieces as having little value.

Shawn's abduction had not become any less important; Taylor would have to face the consequences. But the discovery of his involvement with an international theft ring stirred Shawn's anxiety. The artifacts had been found over fifty years earlier, and now they were safely hidden in the Kellys' basement. It seemed that no one knew anything about them, or that they even existed, and no one had come forth making any claims to them. Although the

FBI considered their significance rather minimal, Shawn was certain they were more than just worthless hunks of metal, and he wondered how long it would be until another adversary would attempt to bargain, blackmail, or steal.

Hardly a day had passed without a probing journalist dropping in at the library. Shawn's identity was known around the world, and the global fixation that Taylor's thievery had attracted, concerned Shawn. He had given his story to so many strangers, and now he was beginning to think that had been a mistake. He didn't know whom to trust any more.

"Call Sorenson," Steve suggested.

"What good will that do?"

"Maybe he can give you some advice."

Shawn dug the FBI agent's card from his wallet and dialed the number.

"I don't know that you can change any of that, now," Bill Sorenson responded to Shawn's concern. "Just be careful who you talk to... make them show credentials... or, learn how to say no. In time, they'll stop coming around."

"Okay," Shawn said, just a little disappointed.

"Oh. And by the way," Sorenson added. "There was one inquiry about the artifacts... from some scientists in France."

Shawn recalled the letter he had found in Taylor's briefcase; he knew what the Frenchmen wanted, without asking, but he asked anyway. "What did they want?"

"We were a little suspicious of them at first, so we conducted an investigation."

"And what did you find out?"

"Seems the group of French archaeologists are legitimate. We couldn't find any connection to the thefts. They aren't interested in Taylor – just the artifacts, and because we can't control what the newspapers print, they know who you are, and probably where to find you."

"What makes them think I have the artifacts?"

"Shawn, just between you and me... I think you know where they are."

"What makes *you* think that?"

"Well, because Steve is the only person who knew where the box was. He had the key to the locker, and there's some time that morning that we can't account for."

Shawn hesitated. He didn't have an answer.

"Personally, Shawn," Sorenson continued, "I don't care if you have them. It's like money recovered and returned. They're yours."

"So, are the French scientists coming here?" Shawn asked.

"They might."

CHAPTER 19

A few nights after his talk with Bill Sorenson, Shawn was eager to resume the artifact study. Steve had taken on a more active role in the research, too, and having been tipped off on the French scientists' possible arrival, they felt as if they had entered into a race to discover the secret. Surely, the foreign scientists were more experienced, and they had more resources, but Shawn and Steve were convinced that, with all five pieces, instead of just four, they were leaving the Frenchmen in the dust.

Steve's theory of mathematic values holding some significance differed from Shawn's idea that an intellectual message was more likely, although, neither totally disagreed with the other. The inconsistency of the markings contrasted with the precise sameness of the wedges, each one claiming exactly 72 degrees of the complete circle, and each one, identically sectioned by the arced, parallel lines. Shawn concurred that numbers were a perceivable factor; he was stalled on the number five.

Sara's notes didn't indicate her pursuit leading to anything beyond logic; she had followed a hard line from one time period to another, and another. Her notes rambled from the Egyptians to the Incas to the Vikings, and nothing conclusive. Logic had taken her nowhere, and it was only elevating Shawn's frustrations; he thought it was time to explore another avenue – *the illogical*. He had a hunch, based on his recollections of some previous school research project. It remained doubtful that any solid proof would surface; solid proof didn't seem to exist, but, perhaps, some sort of reasonable association would appear.

Shawn ambled off to a remote library corner in search of a reference book, the title of which he didn't recall, but he vaguely remembered the material in it. If his hunches were correct, the book would reveal an association that had been simmering in his subconscious mind. The book contained the writings of Plato, the ancient Greek philosopher. He recalled, too, that the book also included modern-day, analytical, scientific validity of actual historic values, and reports of recent archaeological follow-up expeditions.

Mid-way down the aisle, Shawn stopped in his tracks. A gray-haired woman stood at the far end with her back to him. He couldn't recall anyone coming in, and he hadn't noticed anyone moving about, even if she had entered undetected. "Can I help you find something?" he asked quietly.

The woman in the turquoise dress turned toward Shawn. Her pixy face smiled warmly, like only Sara could, but she said nothing. Her left hand rose slowly to the shelf and came to rest gracefully on a book spine.

Shawn wanted to speak, but he couldn't. Sara was there, and he knew that he must be witnessing a mirage, or, perhaps, his imagination was just running wild. He closed his eyes tightly and wished that Sara were really standing at the end of the aisle.

"This is the book you're looking for, Shawn," he heard Sara's voice say, and he opened his eyes. Sara faded into a haze, and then vanished.

Shawn smiled inside. He knew Sara could never leave this library that she loved so dearly, and she would still be there to help him with his projects… always.

He stepped slowly to the spot where Sara had been. He looked at the shelf where her hand had pointed. One book was pulled a few inches out from the others, and it *was* the one he had tried to remember.

Steve sensed that Shawn was onto something when he returned to the reading table with a thick hard cover book. Shawn's eyes scanned the pages briskly. Steve wanted to ask what he had found, but he knew he shouldn't interrupt Shawn's intense concentration.

Shawn stopped reading, grabbed the pencil from Steve's grasp, and tapped the eraser end on his chin a few times while staring, deeply in thought. After a few seconds, he put the pencil to a blank sheet of paper and began drawing a large five-point star, as if a brainstorm were consuming him. "We've been looking at the wedges all wrong," he said.

"What d'ya mean?" Steve peered at the drawing, puzzled by Shawn's renewed enthusiasm.

Shawn realized that Steve needed some background. He pushed the paper aside and slid the open book in front of him again, flipping back a few pages. "Listen to this," he said, and began reading aloud:

> *"At the beginning of the world, Poseidon, God of the Sea, was given the island continent as his share of the earth."*

"Whoa, Sherlock," Steve blurted. "Poseidon… that's from Greek Mythology! I thought we were—"

"Now just hold on, Watson," Shawn interrupted. "This will explain a few things… the number five, the strange metal, the precision…"

"Okay, okay… I'm listening. Read on."

Shawn continued reading from the book:

> *"The land was abundant with food and pure water, animals and forest. The soil was rich, and* precious metals *and all other minerals were plentiful. It was truly a paradise... Within a short time, Poseidon fell in love with Cleito, a mortal maiden of the island, and to protect her, he created* five alternate rings *of water and land in perfect circles around the hill where she resided... Cleito bore him* five *sets of male twins... Poseidon divided up the land between his ten sons, and each became the ruler of their segments. Atlas, the first-born of the eldest twins, became the first Chief King of the entire land, and it was he who gave the dynasty its name. As the population grew over time, the people evolved into a highly skilled and talented civilization, and developed*

technology far ahead of the times, including travel and trade with other civilizations around the world."

Shawn paused and glanced across the table at Steve's one raised eyebrow. Obviously, Steve hadn't heard enough to grasp the concept. "There's more," Shawn explained. He turned a couple of pages, thinking he should tell Steve about his vision of Sara, but convincing Steve that he had just seen a ghost would only complicate the issue further. Convincing him that numerous facts would substantiate a mere hunch was a great enough task. He continued with summaries of other related material from the book:

"Geologists, in a scientific manner, believe that if Atlantis really did exist, its destruction was the result of catastrophic natural disasters -- earthquakes, volcanic eruptions, and tidal waves. However, there is an ever-growing number of 'Atlantists' who have been studying the legends, and have mounted a search for this lost land. There are those who believe they have discovered evidence that the Atlanteans had developed such advanced technology as lasers, aircraft, television, death rays, and atomic energy, as this civilization included people who were skillful metallurgists and engineers. It is also believed, by some, that Atlantis' destruction was not caused by geological events, but instead, by the misuse of the powerful forces they had developed -- perhaps an atomic explosion."

Both of Steve's eyebrows were raised as Shawn glanced in his direction again. He hoped Steve wouldn't abandon him now, on an island of seemingly absurd notions. To Shawn, the concept appeared quite feasible; the number five suddenly appeared as a significant factor -- not once, but *twice*. The excerpts certainly suggested the possibility of some exotic metal, the degree of precision with which the wedges were made, and how they could have reached different parts of the world. He realized that he might be a little premature, jumping to any conclusions, but a gut feeling told him that all the coincidences were pointing to the solution, no matter how far-fetched it might seem.

Steve conceded that there were definitely some parallels -- the number five, the metals, and the technology. But he still had some doubts. "There's never been anything proven that Atlantis really existed...it's mostly just a myth."

"That's what they thought about the City of Troy, too," Shawn retorted. He fumbled for another page in the book. "It says, right here:

"In 1871, Heinrich Schliemann, a German archaeologist, discovered the remains of Troy in Western Turkey, proving *that at least one of the Greek Myths was*

based on historical fact."

"Okay. Atlantis could have been a real place," Steve finally agreed. "But if the wedges had any possible origin there, how did they survive thousands of years? And how did they get into a church attic in Wisconsin?"

Shawn stared off into space. "I don't know."

Steve pulled the paper and pencil across the table and added the arced lines to Shawn's drawing.

"You see?" Shawn said. "In that pattern, the lines that looked like a spider web before, are now perfect circles."

Steve studied the alternate configuration. "What d'ya suppose they signify?"

"I'd bet they represent the rings of water."

The wheels started turning in Steve's head; he recalled the reflected images and the peculiar energy the wedges emitted, and how that energy seemed stronger when the five pieces were together. "They're like batteries," he mumbled, and then he explained his theory to Shawn. "We probably don't need to shine a light on them at all. They've got their own power stored inside… like a battery."

Shawn understood the principle of a battery, but he questioned Steve's reasoning. "But there's no switch to turn it on."

"Doesn't have to be," Steve answered. "When they're arranged in the proper order… like batteries in series… they probably create a magnetic field that activates whatever is inside them."

"Yeah, you're probably right," Shawn agreed. "Now, all we have to do is find the right combination."

****

Shawn opened the library at five o'clock on Friday afternoon. Nothing had changed in his daily routine for a while, and being Friday, he looked forward to eight o'clock, when he and Steve would join Don, Kathy, Richard and Jan at the Old Country Inn for supper. Hardly anyone ever came to the library on Friday nights, and the next three hours would seem like an eternity.

Old Mrs. Clark waddled through the door just as Shawn was getting settled at his desk. She was there to return the parakeet book; it was considerably overdue.

"So, how's your parakeet doing?" Shawn asked.

"Oh. I've taught him to recite the alphabet," Mrs. Clark replied. "Now, if only I could teach him to spell."

Shawn's attention was drawn to an unfamiliar man entering the front door. Steve followed a few steps behind.

"Okay, Mrs. Clark," Shawn said, trying to avoid any further conversation about an alphabet-reciting bird. "Don't worry about the overdue fee. I'll forget it this time."

"Well, thank you, Shawn." Mrs. Clark laid the book on the desktop, turned, and waddled toward the door.

Steve wandered off to the magazine rack across the room, leaving Shawn and the stranger staring at each other. Shawn thought the man was surely just another journalist prodding into his personal life.

"You must be Shawn Kelly," the stranger blurted in a French accent.

Shawn nodded.

The stranger introduced himself: "I am Claude LeFluer. I represent a team of French archaeologists. My colleagues and I have been following your story very closely."

Shawn glanced over his shoulder to see if Steve was taking in the conversation; he appeared to be engrossed in the latest issue of *Popular Mechanix* magazine.

"We associated the news releases with our contact with Professor Woodrow Taylor—"

"Taylor's in jail now," Shawn interrupted.

"Yes, I am aware of that," LeFluer replied. "We learned of his dastardly deeds in news broadcasts on the BBC."

Shawn concluded that if the French scientists had followed the news, they certainly knew about the artifacts and the FBI's suspicions regarding their disappearance; it had been in all of the newspapers. "So, why are you here?" he asked. He knew what the Frenchman wanted, but he wasn't about to volunteer anything.

"My colleagues uncovered four artifacts in a church that was destroyed during World War Two. Professor Taylor contacted us with information about similar pieces found in a church, here in America. We corresponded with him further -- then his replies suddenly stopped. A short time later, we heard about your abduction, and from the photographs of the artifacts that were to be the ransom, we knew they were the missing link to our research."

"So, you have the photographs?"

"They are helpful, but we'd greatly appreciate the real thing."

"Not so fast, Frenchy." Steve stepped between Shawn and LeFluer, as if protecting a little brother from a bully. "What makes you think Shawn has the artifacts?"

Claude's bold approach quickly diminished to meekness; his eyes widened at the sight of Steve's intimidating muscular physique. "Mr. Sorenson of the FBI said that Shawn might know where to find them."

Shawn was glad that Steve had intervened; it gave him a few seconds to think about Agent Sorenson's advice on saying no. "And if I say no," Shawn interrupted, " are you going to kidnap me next week?"

"Heavens! No," Claude said. "We're scientists, not kidnappers. We're on the brink of one of the most notorious discoveries in the history of mankind. It may rate up there with the Dead Sea Scrolls and Noah's Ark. We only seek your help."

The thought had crossed LeFluer's mind to devise a method to obtain the artifacts, but he quickly dismissed that idea; he realized that the young Americans were one step ahead, and from the accounts of the abduction, clever ransom drop, and rescue, they were quite capable of defending something so important to them.

"Tell ya what, Frenchy," Steve said. "Leave your name and address. If they turn up, we'll let ya know."

Claude had endured sweltering heat in the Egyptian deserts, and had risked his life on the mountaintops of Tibet; he was determined, but never before had he encountered the likes of Shawn Kelly and Steve Allison. He wasn't prepared for a confrontation; he retrieved a business card from his pocket and handed it to Shawn.

Shawn and Steve watched from the doorway as Claude LeFluer drove off in the rented Chevrolet. In a few hours, he would be on a flight back to Paris, and they hoped he was the last of the artifact seekers. Everyone who had been a threat was now either in jail, in a foreign country, or no longer interested.

****

It was the first time since before the abduction that Shawn had been to the Old Country Inn for a Friday night supper. And it was the first time that he and Steve had entered that place together. Time had jaded the popularity of the hottest gossip in town, but they both still felt like lumps in a melting pot. Curious stares poked at them from every corner of the crowded dining room as they took their seats at the table with Don and Kathy, Richard and Jan.

After the waitress had taken their orders, Shawn and Steve exchanged stares across the table when Don asked, "Did that foreigner find you at the library this afternoon?"

Shawn didn't want to openly talk about the artifacts in public, and he wasn't sure if his dad even knew they were in the house. "Y-yeah, he did."

Kathy and Jan had been engaged in a discussion about their latest recipe experiments, but Kathy quickly tuned in on the father/son conversation. "I hope you're going to get rid of those things in the basement. It's kind of creepy just knowing they're down there."

Shawn glanced around to the people at the nearest tables, hoping that his mother's voice hadn't carried too far. "Shhhhhh... we're about to make a discovery..." Shawn whispered. He double-checked the nearest tables again to make sure no one was eavesdropping. "... That could be one of the most notorious discoveries in the history of the world."

"Yeah," Steve joined in the whispered conversation. "It could rate right up there with the Dead Sea Scrolls and Noah's Ark."

"So, does that mean you're going to be rich and famous?" Don laughed. "I don't know how much more of that we can handle."

Shawn leaned back in his chair and thought about his dad's sarcastic remark. Even though it was meant as sarcasm, his dad was right. After the weeks of national public exposure, and all the effort required to maintain privacy, Shawn was beginning to think that the quiet life of two-by-fours and ten-penny nails in a small midwestern town might not be so bad, after all. But the renewed perspective wouldn't stop him from continuing the search for an answer to Sara's secret. "Fame is not my priority, Dad. The French scientists can have their glory. I'm just doing this for Sara."

The waitress delivered the food. Kathy and Jan continued their gossip. Don and Richard planned a future fishing trip. Shawn and Steve just ate and listened. Nothing more was said about the artifacts.

When the supper was finished, Don announced the plans for the rest of the evening: "There's a good polka band playing at the *Avalon*. We're going dancing. What are you boys doing tonight?"

"Um… we're just gonna hang out at home."

CHAPTER 20

Not much was said during the drive home. When Shawn eased the Mustang into the driveway and parked in front of the garage door, Steve sat quietly, staring through the windshield. "I've been having these strange visions all day," he said, without breaking his stare.

"What kind of visions?" Shawn asked.

"It's kinda hard to explain, exactly. I keep seeing a table against a blank wall, but it's all so dark and I can't make out anything else."

Shawn jerked his head toward Steve. "I've had visions like that, too. But I see two people sitting by the table."

"Who are they?"

"Don't know for sure. But I think it's us."

"S'pose it has something to do with the artifacts?"

Shawn leaned back in the seat. "Remember when we first got them? Remember when I said that I thought they were trying to communicate with me?"

"Yeah."

"Well, I think we've both received some sort of message from them, and our subconscious minds are just starting to sort it out."

"Then, maybe that's how we're s'posed to look at them… on a table against a bare wall… in the dark."

No more conversation was necessary. They were convinced that their conceptual visions had been transmitted to them, somehow, as a sort of instruction manual. It was worth a try.

Shawn led the way down the basement steps, past the laundry room, furnace, and his dad's workbench, to a room that was used for nothing more than storing unused furniture. He pointed to an old dining table in the corner, and then went back to a shelf behind the furnace where he had hidden the box containing the artifacts.

The storage room was mostly dark; only a little light spilled in from the open doorway, but enough to manage the artifact arrangement on the table. In the stillness of that abyss, the tingling sensation from the mysterious energy, more powerful, now, than they had ever experienced before, produced an eerie ambiance, almost to the point of frightening; even in near darkness, the pieces emitted a faint, hazy glow. An invisible force stirred the air, just barely noticeable, and a sound much like electricity zinging through power lines hummed for just a few seconds, and then died to complete silence.

Shawn and Steve had exposed themselves to an element of danger; there was no one else near to rescue them from catastrophe, should one occur. But they had come so far, and the experience was so incredible, so alluring, so exhilarating. They couldn't stop now, no matter how vulnerable they were to risk; no matter how forbidding the circumstances seemed; no matter how treacherous their next move. They were venturing into a precarious unknown, and they craved the thrill of it all.

Shawn's brow wrinkled with a determined frown; he reached toward the star, reluctantly testing one of its points with a cautious, one-finger tap, and then boldly grasped the piece, lifting it away from the formation. "Switch this one with that one," he whispered to Steve, and pointed to another part of the star.

With the same reluctance, Steve carefully picked up the wedge from the opposite side; they traded pieces, and placed them back in the empty spaces. Nothing different happened; the glow and the hum returned, and then faded. Several more interchanges were tried, all producing the same results.

Steve stared at the glowing star. "I wonder how we'll know when we have the right combination."

"Somehow, I think we'll just know," Shawn said. "Let's try some more."

Again, and again they swapped the wedges to alternate positions. After what seemed to be a hundred moves, they pulled away two adjacent pieces and slowly slid them back into reversed positions. As the pieces were about to make contact, a buzzing, electric blue light arced between their corners. Steve flinched, but his fingertips remained in control of the piece. Shawn pulled his hands away quickly. His entire body abruptly retreated as far as the chair backrest allowed.

"Whoa!" Steve chuckled. "Did you see that?" He swiftly nudged into place the piece Shawn had dropped.

"Yeah," Shawn said, his voice crackling. "I saw that." And then his eyes widened at the view on the table. The hum erupted again, but then changed pitch to a sound resembling the wind whistling through a tunnel. Gradually growing spikes of multi-colored light began shooting toward the ceiling and wall at various angles, some remaining stationary, and some pivoting about, like miniature searchlights. A hazy fog released from the star and hung in the air over the table; the lights intensified and increased in number, and eventually created a solid wall of rainbow-like color within the fog.

Shawn leaned in closer again. "What do you think it is?" He was numb with intrigue.

Steve waved his open palm through the brilliantly colored light. "I don't know. Kinda looks like a test pattern on a TV."

The light faded and brightened a few times, and then it began to take on depth, creating a distorted three-dimensional effect, the colors blending and forming distinct patches and bands of assorted hues. As the depth swelled and advanced toward them, Shawn and Steve cowered away, inching backward into their chairs. An image was slowly forming, but in those early stages, they couldn't distinguish its definition. Intrigue turned to fear as the image encroached upon their space, and the alien atmosphere soon engulfed them.

The image slowly came into focus; it was as if they were viewing a movie screen, but they seemed to be within the picture, totally surrounded by fluffy, white clouds, their viewpoint from far above the earth, looking down onto a mammoth island, amid an ocean of brilliant blues and greens caressing its white sand beaches. As the picture zoomed in closer to the landscape, a dreamy symphonic crescendo flourished to perfection. Steve's fear subsided, and Shawn, too, soon realized they didn't seem to be in any danger.

As if they were aboard a slow-moving aircraft skimming just above the treetops, Shawn and Steve beheld the stunning panorama; miles of lush forest and vast expanses of verdant plains sprawled before them, and colorful birds soared the sky. They passed over cultivated farmland, bountiful orchards, lakes and streams, roads, and tiny hamlets of meticulous homes with manicured lawns and gardens.

"What is this place?" Steve whispered, just loud enough to be heard over the music.

Immersed in paralyzing amazement, Shawn just shook his head slowly, unable to respond verbally. The most sensational view they had ever experienced became more incredible as the life-like, three-dimensional image moved them toward the center of the island.

They were approaching the rolling foothills of a larger mountain, covered with lavish foliage, interrupted by sporadic, multi-colored rock cliffs. As the mountain drew nearer and the smaller hills no longer hid its base from view, a wide canal of water came into sight; it seemed to encircle the mountain. Then a second canal, and a third, circled the mountain, like the rings around Saturn. Between them lay acres of cropland, scattered with houses and barns connected by trails.

High on the mountain's plateau there appeared to be a city; sunray tangents sparking off in a thousand directions from golden rooftops suggested that this was never-never land.

Steve leaned into Shawn's shoulder and whispered; "I don't think we're in Kansas, anymore."

Shawn acknowledged the whimsical quip, but then his seriousness took over again. "It's just like Plato described." Scanning the spectacular vista, eyes wide with intrigue, he absorbed every detail, but he didn't elaborate his statement any further.

Boats upon the shimmering canals passed beneath them as the picture zoomed in on the city. Like the tiles on a scrabble board, the city was a network of flat-roofed structures, intermingled with well-groomed gardens, courtyards, pools of crystal-clear water, and fountains. At the very center stood a luxurious temple with enormous white marble pillars supporting a gold-covered roof that glistened in the sunlight.

While Shawn studied the city's architecture, Steve's attention was drawn to a tower constructed of alternating red and white blocks. It appeared to have its base at the foot of the mountain, and rose above the plateau, with a bridge linking it to the building complex at the far edge of the city. Steve nudged Shawn with his elbow. "Look at that... a dirigible." He pointed to the dolphin-shaped airship docked at the tower's peak. Then he pointed Shawn's attention to another similar airship that hovered high above the distant outer canal.

The bird's eye view quickly descended to ground level at the center of a courtyard where they were amidst grapevines and trees heavily laden with luscious fruit, and thick, green grass carpeted the soil.

Inhabitants of this utopia wore little or no clothing; they were perfect specimens of human form, cheerful and content, casually strolling about the walkways, uninhibited, as if enjoying a holiday weekend. Some stopped to pluck the succulent fruit from the trees to satisfy their desire for nourishment.

The angelic music faded, giving way to the natural sounds of chirping birds, a gentle breeze fluttering the leaves, murmuring voices and subdued laughter. It all seemed so real that Shawn thought he felt the wind.

Unexpectedly, a pleasant, mellow voice echoed, "Welcome." Shawn and Steve shifted their weight, craning their necks attempting to discover the origin of the greeting.

The strong-but-gentle voice continued as the picture zeroed in on a doorway. "You have arrived here only by virtue of the strong bond between you. Our society was built on that premise -- that all people may prosper by bonding, combining their energy, and attaining ultimate levels of security, technology, and quality of life. We have evolved over thousands of generations to a civilization unequaled anywhere in the world."

Apparently, the voice was narrating a guided tour. Shawn and Steve found themselves emerging from the doorway into a large room where dozens of adolescents, seated at long tables placed in a horseshoe fashion, attentively absorbed wisdom from their teacher at the head of the class.

"From our offspring," the guide voice went on, "we have produced the finest agriculturists, mathematicians, philosophers, teachers, engineers, and scientists, the results of which, you are about to see in all its magnificent splendor."

The tour continued, moving through the entrance to another extravagant room large enough to contain a stadium. "This is the Hall of Archives," the voice explained. "Every accomplishment of our people, great and small, is recorded here. Nearly every day, our quality of life is enhanced, and with each improvement, a permanent installation is added to these archives."

Shawn marveled at the vast library of books and documents; Steve's intrigue was captured by the countless displays of mechanical ingenuity. As they were guided through the great hall, every imaginable form of technology appeared in overwhelmingly abundant proportions.

The journey extended into what appeared to be an elaborate celestial observatory. The walls enshrined hundreds of planetary charts and pictures, as if the solar system were the essence of a religion. The place was deserted now, but the voice embellished: "When darkness falls upon our land, and the heavens enlighten us with the visions of distant worlds, this facility will be alive with our fascination to explore those worlds. We believe the Gods are calling us to them."

Leaving the scholastic environment behind, the tour ushered Shawn and Steve to view the proletariat; this society did include a working class. Laborers toiled in the fields, vineyards and orchards, harvesting grains, vegetables and fruit; factories and workshops hummed with production and in shipyards along the canals, the manufactured goods and food products were readied for transport to domestic and foreign destinations. Nowhere were there any signs of discontent; the labor force seemed to enjoy their work, and although this society appeared to be quite industrious, there was no evidence of commercialism or greed.

The journey went on to view miles of tranquility amidst the tropical forest where leopard-like cats basked lazily in patches of sunlight, and exotic birds of every color decorated the trees like Christmas ornaments. Just beyond the jungle shadows, herds of white-tailed deer grazed in velvety green meadows. Waterfalls tumbled gracefully from granite-laden hillsides to placid valley lakes.

Voyaging on, Shawn and Steve were guided over winding mountain trails to view grand paradise vistas and along white sandy ocean beaches dotted with tide pools that marked the boundaries of utopia, and finally came full circle to their starting point within the citadel.

Before them stood a magnificent temple, its glittering stone walls recessed under a golden roof supported by white marble pillars. Once again the angelical music was heard softly, and the guide voice spoke: "We were born a peaceful and loving people, rising from the loins of Poseidon, who still watches over us and protects us. But our civilization is now threatened by an inevitable force -- one which Poseidon himself can offer no defense. The weaker members of our society have fled, exiling themselves to other lands to escape the perils of doom. But those of us with strong beliefs of a divine rite have remained here to face our fate. We prepared the five tablets as an epitaph to our existence, to be discovered long after we perish from this earth. By the essence of your ability to function -- as we do -- you have unlocked the energy of the tablets. Once spent, that energy will be gone forever. Return now, to the security of your own time... and may Poseidon guide you there safely."

The three-dimensional picture that surrounded Shawn and Steve slowly receded to a blurry, distorted, flat image rising above the table. It flickered a couple of times, and then it was gone. All that remained was the hazy cloud, lingering like the smoke after a fireworks grand finale.

The boys sat speechless in the darkened room. Only the light from the open doorway streaked over the floor. Shawn rose from his chair, crossed the room, and reached for the light switch beside the door. Steve squinted as the room brightened. Shawn returned to the table and rested his palms flat on its top. The artifacts' luster had turned to an unattractive dullness; the sparkle that once emitted from the etchings was no longer present. Shawn picked up one of the pieces and held it firmly. Only the feel of a lifeless, cold object filled his hand, and nothing more; the sensational energy was just a memory.

Steve looked on with a curious sort of sadness. He saw the expression of concern painted on his friend's face. "What do you suppose that was that we just saw?" he asked Shawn, his voice, only a whisper.

Shawn stared blankly at the tabletop. "It's just like Plato described. Three water canals protecting a city on top of a mountain." He looked squarely into Steve's eyes and spoke clearly, "Atlantis."

Steve though for a moment. "D'ya think it's for real?"

"Let me ask you this, Watson. Can you think of any other possible explanation for it?"

"It could be..." Steve paused. He didn't have an explanation.

"Sara found these things over fifty years ago," Shawn continued. "No one then had the technology to produce something so incredible as what we just saw."

"Come to think of it," Steve added, "I'm not so sure that anyone has that kind of technology, even now."

Shawn laid the piece on the table. A feeling of despair overwhelmed him. "What have we done?" Guilt flowed with his words; he knew this had been a one-shot deal, and now, his obsession had rendered the artifacts worthless.

Steve laid a hand on Shawn's shoulder. "We've discovered the solution to one of the greatest mysteries of the world," he said, attempting to appease Shawn's guilt.

Shawn looked Steve full in the eyes. "And just *who* is going to believe us?"

CHAPTER 21

"Has the jury reached a unanimous verdict?"

"We have, Your Honor."

The bailiff took the paper from the jury foreman and approached the judge's bench; his heels striking the hardwood floor tapped a steady, precise cadence that echoed through the deathly quiet courtroom. There was a long pause as the judge donned his reading glasses and studied the paper at length.

Shawn sat beside his father at the back of the room filled to near capacity with curious spectators, his hands, clammy with nervous sweat. He had been subpoenaed to testify at the trial that only lasted four hours, and he was thankful that it was over, but now he feared the outcome. His testimony had been brief – only ten minutes – which neither attributed to blame, nor dismissed it. He had merely been asked to describe his actions on that night he discovered Sara lying in a road ditch, and the condition in which he had found her. Mixed emotions were doing battle in his head: his good friend, Sara Fremont, was dead; her life had been cut unjustly short, but it was his uncle, Andy Kelly, who now faced the decision of his guilt or innocence, made by twelve people.

Shawn tried to imagine the pending trial still before him; surely, he would spend hours on the witness stand during Professor Taylor's trial. He didn't look forward to it with any degree of pleasure, but he was thankful, too, that this one had come first; it prepared him for the shocking, preposterous techniques and the theatrical performances delivered by defense lawyers.

In Andy's defense, his attorney had cleverly camouflaged the real issue – Sara's death. He had turned the tide from questioning Andy Kelly's responsibility for the occurrence, to questioning the adeptness of the law enforcement officials performing its investigation. The Sheriff had not properly documented the collection of evidence – he couldn't prove that the cloth fragment had been removed from Andy's car. Nor was there any solid proof, without reasonable doubt, that Andy had driven the car that struck Sara. Another witness had testified that he drove Andy home that night, and that he had found the keys still in the ignition switch when he walked Andy to his car in the parking lot. That only meant that anyone could have taken the Oldsmobile earlier in the evening and returned it without being noticed, and no further investigation had been carried out to determine if there had been another driver at the wheel of Andy's car that night.

Shawn had taken notice of the issues made by the defense; deep down inside, he hoped that tactic would work. His uncle was no model citizen, and perhaps he deserved a generous helping of justice, but he was a blood relative. After all that had happened, Shawn's bitter attitude toward Andy had mellowed – not because he thought Andy was free of guilt, but because Shawn's father had already endured enough humility. The mere thought of being labeled the brother of a convicted criminal would be devastating.

Shawn wondered if Andy had been implicated in the Taylor conspiracy; that issue had not yet come to light, and he certainly had been involved. No matter what this outcome, Andy Kelly's struggle with the law was not over.

The restlessness of the people around him and the judge's voice abruptly earned Shawn's attention.

"In the matter of State versus Andrew Kelly, what say you?"

The bailiff returned the paper to the jury spokesperson as the judge announced his formal request. Andy and his attorney stood, facing the jury as they had been instructed to do; Andy was trembling.

"We find the defendant *not* guilty."

A rumble of voices erupted like the first thunder of a storm. Shawn wasn't sure if the reaction was the result of pleasure with the verdict, or that of disgust.

The judge rapped his gavel once, sending an official proclamation ringing throughout the room. He thanked the jury for their service, and then turned his unsmiling stare toward Andy. "The defendant is free to go."

The cunning performance by the defense attorney had successfully swayed the jury, but Shawn sensed from the judge's stern glare and the tone of his voice that *he* had not been thoroughly convinced.

Shawn drew a deep breath and let out a prolonged sigh. He glanced at his father's expression that projected little more than relief.

Was Andy *really* innocent? Or were the flamboyant attorney's monetary interests and the prestige of victory more valuable to him than discovering the truth? And was the victim's dignity not important? Shawn knew that whatever the answers to those questions were, he would always feel uncomfortable in Andy's presence, and that the absolute truth might never be known.

CHAPTER 22

Only a week remained until Shawn would join his academe at the University. Once there, he would have plenty of time to get settled in, and attend various orientation seminars before the busy class schedule began. But time didn't seem so plentiful now, as there were so many preparations to make. The summer had slipped away, but despite a few interruptions, Shawn looked back upon the last couple of months with little regret. He was a stronger person now that he had been exposed to adversity; he was eager to move forward and to meet the new challenges awaiting him at college.

Jan Williams didn't really need any training as the new librarian; it seemed a bit ironic to Shawn that one of his former teachers would require his assistance, but he agreed to spend a few evenings there with her.

Several people had come and gone that Monday night, and by 7:00 o'clock, Jan was engaged in a gab session with a couple of her school faculty friends. Shawn patiently watched the clock; he and Steve had planned a campout and a few hours of fishing at the lake.

Two men entered the library. Shawn recognized FBI Agent Bill Sorenson, but he had never seen the other man before; he thought the stranger was just another Bureau agent, and this meeting would be the first of many leading up to the legal proceedings against Professor Taylor.

"Hello, Shawn," Sorenson beamed. He reached toward Shawn for a handshake, and then proceeded with an introduction: "Shawn Kelly, this is Mr. George Livingston."

They shook hands. Shawn anticipated that the fishing and camping was about to be ruined. "If this is about—"

"Is there someplace we can talk privately?" Sorenson interrupted.

Shawn glanced toward Jan and her two friends and then guided the men to a table at the other side of the room.

"I thought it would be more appropriate to tell you all this before you read it in the newspapers," Sorenson began.

Shawn threw him a curious stare.

"None of this has been released to the media yet, but by tomorrow at this time, it will be common knowledge to the whole country. That's why we're here tonight."

Shawn leaned forward in his chair. "Is this going to take a long time? If it is, I need to call Steve."

"Not long at all," Sorenson assured. "We'll only be a few minutes."

Shawn leaned back.

"Yesterday, at about four in the afternoon," Sorenson continued, "Woodrow Taylor suffered a massive heart attack, and died in his jail cell. We had our case nearly prepared and ready to go to trial in the matter of your abduction... but now, that trial is never going to happen."

Shawn suddenly felt a tremendous load lift off his shoulders. "But what about the other two guys who helped him?"

"Tommy Abbott, who was arrested at the same time, has given us a full confession, and has waived his right to trial with a plea bargain for lesser charges. His sentencing is next week, and he'll spend the next seven years in a Federal Prison. The third man, Curtis Kastillo, didn't get off so easily. His body was pulled out of the river downstream from the Taylor mansion a couple of weeks ago. It took a while to make a positive identification. Apparently, he tried to escape that night by swimming across the river... he didn't make it."

"So, what'll happen now?" Shawn asked.

"We have found no evidence of anyone else involved in your abduction," Sorenson explained. "And for what it's worth, we have apprehended seventeen people, so far, connected to Taylor's theft ring. But it has been agreed that there is no need to bring you or your friends into any of that, now that Taylor is dead. Seems like your part is done."

Shawn had never felt such overwhelming relief. He had feared the tremendous stress, the disruption of the coming school term, and the plaguing publicity that would not have allowed him to carry on a normal lifestyle. But now, in just a few short minutes, his fears evaporated. He looked at Sorenson with reservation. "You mean... it's all over? Just like that?"

Sorenson smiled and nodded. "Well, except for one little detail that Mr. Livingston will tell you about."

George Livingston hoisted an expensive-looking leather-covered attaché case onto the table. "I am an investigator for a number of large insurance companies. A great deal of valuable art recovered from the Taylor mansion was subject to about three million dollars in pending claims. Thanks to you, most of those items have been returned to the rightful owners." He retrieved an official-looking four-by-ten inch document from his case. "All the insurance companies have contributed to this reward. It gives me great pleasure, Mr. Kelly, to present you with this check." He handed it across the table to Shawn.

Staring at the check in disbelief, Shawn had difficulty in responding. "There... there must be some mistake... this check is for ten thousand dollars."

Mr. Livingston spoke in a matter-of-factly tone. "There's no mistake... it's a modest sum compared to the claims we would have paid, had the property not been recovered. We all agreed that you should be the recipient of the reward."

The youngster still couldn't believe what he was seeing. "Is this really mine? Is this for real?"

"Yes, Mr. Kelly, it is real, and it is yours."

"Well, actually, I have to share this with Steve and Lee. They had just as much to do with it as I did. Maybe more."

Livingston reached over the table and took Shawn's hand. "No, Mr.

Kelly, you don't have to share that with anyone. I have two more checks just like that one... each written to Steve Allison and Lee Krueger."

"Hey Sherlock," Steve's voice cut through the silence. "You ready to go soon?"

Sorenson turned to see Steve standing just inside the front entrance, clutching a sleeping bag and a fishing pole. "Ah! Steve Allison," Sorenson called out. "Would you come over here and sit down, please?"